m

Tunbowfields Library
Tel 01892 53262
Fax 01892 514657
tunbridgewellslibrary@kent.gov.uk

11 - 06

06. DEC 06.

26. OCT 07.

04 MAY 07 21. NOV 07.

17. DEC 07.

12. JUN 07

23. JUL 07

13. OCT 07

29. DEC 08

28. JAN 09

18 JUN 2010

27 JAN 2011

8 FEB 2011

26. APR

Symes K Gould

WITHDRAWN

Books should be returned or renewed by the
last date stamped above

McCuaig, Catriona
Mail order bride

0 5 JUL 2011

CHARTER MARK
CUSTOMER SERVICE EXCELLENCE

Kent
County
Council

Libraries & Archives

C152904615

SPECIAL MESSAGE TO READERS

This book is published under the auspices of

THE ULVERSCROFT FOUNDATION

(registered charity No. 264873 UK)

Established in 1972 to provide funds for research, diagnosis and treatment of eye diseases. Examples of contributions made are: —

A Children's Assessment Unit at
Moorfield's Hospital, London.

•

Twin operating theatres at the
Western Ophthalmic Hospital, London.

•

A Chair of Ophthalmology at the
Royal Australian College of Ophthalmologists.

•

The Ulverscroft Children's Eye Unit at the
Great Ormond Street Hospital For Sick Children,
London.

You can help further the work of the Foundation by making a donation or leaving a legacy. Every contribution, no matter how small, is received with gratitude. Please write for details to:

THE ULVERSCROFT FOUNDATION,
The Green, Bradgate Road, Anstey,
Leicester LE7 7FU, England.
Telephone: (0116) 236 4325

In Australia write to:
THE ULVERSCROFT FOUNDATION,
c/o The Royal Australian and New Zealand
College of Ophthalmologists,
94-98 Chalmers Street, Surry Hills,
N.S.W. 2010, Australia

MAIL ORDER BRIDE

Lydia McFarlane has been used to a life of wealth and privilege, but when her father remarries, her new stepmother starts a systematic campaign to remove Lydia from the family home in Ontario, plotting to marry her off to a man who doesn't love her. Lydia decides to take matters into her own hands, and runs away to the prairie town of Alberta to become a mail order bride — but life in the Golden West is not as idyllic as Lydia has imagined . . .

Books by Catriona McCuaig
in the Linford Romance Library:

ICE MAIDEN

CATRIONA McCUAIG

---◆---

MAIL ORDER BRIDE

Complete and Unabridged

LINFORD
Leicester

First published in Great Britain in 2005

First Linford Edition
published 2006

Copyright © 2005 by Catriona McCuaig
All rights reserved

British Library CIP Data

McCuaig, Catriona, 1938 –
    Mail order bride.—Large print ed.—
Linford romance library
1. Mail order brides—Fiction
2. Frontier and pioneer life—Alberta—
Fiction 3. Love stories 4. Large type books
I. Title
823.9'14 [F]

ISBN 1–84617–531–3

KENT
ARTS & LIBRARIES

C\ 5 2 9 0 4 6 1 5

Published by
F. A. Thorpe (Publishing)
Anstey, Leicestershire

Set by Words & Graphics Ltd.
Anstey, Leicestershire
Printed and bound in Great Britain by
T. J. International Ltd., Padstow, Cornwall

This book is printed on acid-free paper

1

Lydia McFarlane stared at the letter in disbelief. Apart from one or two ink blots it was nicely written, almost poetical. The man seemed to have had some sort of education, unlike some of the settlers in the Canadian West. Furthermore, it appeared that he spoke English, which was a plus.

The new immigrants came from all parts of Europe and it was only to be expected that they had their own languages — the Norwegians, the Ukrainians, the Danes and all the rest. But if Lydia was going to marry a farmer and spend the rest of her life under the same roof with him, they must be able to communicate, so an English-speaking man it had to be, although if necessary she could get by with her schoolgirl French.

However, it wasn't that this Joseph

Dunfield was able to correspond in correct English that caused her amazement. It was the fact that he wanted her to pack her bags and go out to join him in Alberta, and had enclosed money for her to purchase a one-way train ticket.

Dear Miss McFarlane, the letter said in part, *I have received your letter of the fifteenth inst., and have perused it with great interest. From what you have to say you should suit me very well, and therefore I ask that you will do me the honour of agreeing to become my wife.*

At this time of year I have neither the time nor the inclination to travel East, but we can be married in town when you arrive on the train and before I bring you home to the farm.

The writer went on to describe his farm; the acreage, the number of cattle he owned and the furnishings in his home. None of it meant much to Lydia, who was rather lacking in imagination when it came to places she had never seen. She had an idea that the prairie was an endless expanse of land, but that was so different from the old city of Kingston, Ontario, where she had lived all her life, that it might as well have been the moon.

Alberta, formerly part of what was known as the North West Territory, had become a province in its own right in 1905, and according to what one read in the newspapers, it would grow quickly and prosper.

Some sort of elegant society would emerge in time, but possibly without the rigid conventions she was used to. It would be the perfect setting for the upcoming generation, the makings of a new world. But that was all in the future. The most important thing was that she was holding a proposal of marriage in her hand, and if she made up her mind to accept it, all her problems would be solved.

Kingston, situated on the shores of Lake Ontario, Canada, was founded in the seventeenth century, sometimes called the limestone city because of its many fine stone buildings. It was in one of the better stone houses that Lydia was born and brought up.

Her father, Alexander McFarlane, had made his money as a railway promoter and his family lived a life of wealth and privilege alongside others of their class. When Lydia was fifteen, her mother died, and when the funeral was over, her father explained that the running of the house would now be in her hands.

'Not that it will be hard to do,' he told her, smiling benignly at his woebegone little daughter in her black mourning clothes. 'It is merely a matter of keeping the servants in order.'

When she responded with a squeak of fright he patted her on the head and said, 'Good practice for when you get married and have a home of your own to oversee. In the meantime, I shall, of course, need a hostess at my dinner parties and so on, and I shall be pleased to show off my lovely daughter.'

He was right, of course. The servants, loyal to dear Mrs McFarlane, were on their mettle to help Miss Lydia, and after a few false starts she grew into her rôle as housekeeper and began to enjoy herself.

The years slipped by, and Kingston Society became used to seeing Alexander McFarlane accompanied by his pretty daughter at the dinner parties and balls to which he was always invited as an eligible single man.

It was with a sense of shock, then, that Lydia became aware that change was in the air. A particular dinner party was in the offing, and she was making up place cards in a careful copperplate hand. These would be displayed in the little china holders used for the purpose. Guest list in hand, Lydia found her father in his study, smoking a cigar.

'Who is Miss Holmwood, Papa? I shan't know where to seat her at table.'

Was she mistaken, or did he turn slightly pink around the ears?

'Miss Thea Holmwood, Lydia.'

'Yes, but who is she?'

'She and her brother are new in town. They are from Toronto. He is a lawyer who has joined McTavish & Flyte.'

Lydia looked at the guest list.

'You haven't written him down and the numbers seem to be even,' she began, and was surprised when her father frowned and waved an impatient hand at her.

'I'm giving this party to introduce Miss Holmwood to our friends,' he snapped. 'And you may seat her at my right hand. That's all you need to know.'

Lydia left him, bewildered. Later that day, her friend, Cassandra Evans, called, and Lydia told her what had been said. Cassandra hesitated.

'Well, I don't want to say the wrong thing, Lydia, but rumour has it that your father has been seen in public with Miss Holmwood on several occasions recently. In fact, I saw them together at the theatre the other evening.'

Lydia felt slightly hurt. She had been

her father's companion for so long, it seemed queer if he was going out and about with someone else. Cassandra was looking at her friend strangely.

'I do hope I haven't spoken out of turn, Lydia. I suppose we all assumed that he would have told you about his association with her, especially if . . . ' She broke off, biting her lip.

'If what, Cassie?'

'Well, if he means to marry her, I suppose.'

Lydia gasped. It had never crossed her mind that her father might wish to remarry some day. He had loved her mother, she was sure. But now she recalled a scrap of conversation she had overheard at a party, between two older ladies who had stopped talking abruptly when she entered the room.

'Still a young man . . . eligible . . . every man wants a son, of course.'

Had they meant Alexander McFarlane, her father?

Later, walking home along the lake shore, Lydia tried to come to terms with these new ideas. Perhaps she was being selfish. Having a daughter as a companion and hostess was not the same thing as a wife, she supposed. And perhaps Papa did want more children, in particular, sons to follow him in business. She must try to see his point of view, and she would do her best to welcome Miss Holmwood into the family, if that proved to be necessary.

'So, what is she like?' Cassie wanted to know, when they met the morning after the dinner party.

Lydia pulled a face.

'I hardly know. She was very stiff with me, I thought, but all sweetness and light with Papa, hanging on his every word.'

'I don't suppose she meant anything by it, her manner toward you, I mean. I expect she feels rather shy. After all, you and your father have been so dependent on each other since your mother died. She may be afraid that you'll be resentful.'

Lydia wasn't so sure. There had been

a hard look in Miss Holmwood's eyes, the sort of expression that said, 'Don't you dare try to cross me, or you'll be sorry.'

She obviously didn't try that expression on Alexander McFarlane, though. He bestowed on her the sort of doting look that Lydia hadn't seen since she was a small child, when she had earned his praise for some particular action or achievement.

Cassie smiled.

'I shouldn't worry, Lydia. After all, you're almost twenty years old, so she can hardly send you to your room without your supper. And you'll be leaving the house to get married one of these days, in any case.'

'Married!' Lydia scoffed. 'I don't have hordes of suitors lining up to propose to me. Not like you, Cassie!'

Cassie blushed. She was in love with a young man who was in training at the nearby Royal Military College. Lydia loved to tease her friend about the fact that she was probably in love with his smart red uniform rather than Colin himself. Privately, she thought that he was rather dull and stuffy, but she couldn't tell Cassie that!

In due course, what Lydia had feared came about. She had to sit attentively in St George's Cathedral, with a fixed smile on her face, watching her father being joined in matrimony to Thea Holmwood.

'He looks absolutely besotted,' she told herself sourly. 'As for her, does she have to look quite so triumphant? Anyone would think she was marrying Royalty.'

At the reception which followed, most people avoided the subject of how the marriage might affect Lydia, all but one brash lady who brayed like a donkey and said, 'Now your nose will be out of joint, miss, eh?'

Lydia smiled weakly and murmured something non-committal in reply. What happened next was something of an anti-climax, as the bridal pair went off on a tour of Europe for their honeymoon. Lydia resumed her usual tasks as housekeeper, and prepared to enjoy a quiet life. Time enough to worry about the future when her father and stepmother returned to Canada.

2

Your bedroom, Lydia,' Thea McFarlane said soon after their return from their honeymoon. 'I understand that it was always your parents' room when your mother was alive.'

'That's right. After Mother died, Papa decided that he didn't want to sleep there any more, so we exchanged.'

Lydia loved the high-ceilinged room with its tall, casement windows, over-looking the lake. The furniture was just as it was when her mother had used the room. Lydia could remember seeing her mother seated at the dressing-table, getting ready to come down to dinner, or to go out for the evening, and now her own gowns hung in the wardrobe which had once held Helene McFarlane's things.

Thea looked scornfully at this furniture now.

'Alex and I can't possibly share that poky little room across the hall, Lydia. I'm sure you can see that. This is much more suitable for the master bedroom. I shall have your things moved across the hall tomorrow morning. In the meantime, perhaps you will pack up all this bric-a-brac so the servants will have less to do.'

Lydia tried hard to keep her temper down.

'I'm sorry, Thea. I prefer to stay here. It was my own mother's room, you see. Everything here reminds me of her, the wallpaper, the curtains, the paintings. Nothing has been changed since she died.'

It was the wrong thing to say. Thea's nostrils flared.

'We'll see what your father has to say about this,' she snapped, as she swept out of the room.

Unfortunately, what Alexander McFarlane had to say was no comfort to his daughter.

'Thea is my wife now, Lydia. Her

wishes have to be considered. After all, she is mistress of my home now. Be a good girl and do as she asks. If you don't want to take back your old room, I'll let you choose one of the other bedrooms. The Blue Room, for instance. It's almost as big and it has a pretty view of the orchard.'

Lydia thanked him and decided not to say any more. This was an argument she couldn't win so there was no point in stirring up trouble.

Within days, a team of decorators had been called in, and the familiar old wallpaper was stripped off and the curtains burned.

'They were full of moths,' Thea insisted when Lydia argued that she'd wanted them transferred to her new room.

There were other, smaller pinpricks. Now it was Thea, not Lydia, who sat at the other end of the long, polished dining table when guests came. This was only right, of course, but did Lydia always have to be placed next to the least interesting guest, such as deaf old Colonel Emerson? It was impossible to talk to him so she had to sit quietly and listen to the scintillating conversation that flowed all around her, for to shout at him would have been unladylike.

Thea insisted on approving all the menus, and was perfectly within her rights to do so, except that she would keep ordering things which Lydia hated, and allowing no substitutes.

The cushions in her father's study were rather worn and faded, and Lydia decided to make new covers. The study was his domain alone, so surely she wouldn't be encroaching on Thea's preserves if she did this. She chose a pretty but complicated Jacobean design, which she was working in autumn colours on beige linen. She told herself that if she worked hard she could finish the first one in time for his birthday, and would be able to complete one or two more for Christmas.

'What are you working on, dear?' Thea asked one evening and took the work from Lydia's hands, gazing at it critically.

'It's a cushion cover for Papa's birthday. I'm quite pleased with the way it's turning out. I believe he'll like it.'

Thea wrinkled her nose.

'That sort of thing is a bit passé, don't you think? Go on with it by all means, but use it on the couch in your own room. Let me be the judge of what is best for your father. I'll order a new set of cushions immediately. Crushed velvet, I think, in a masculine-looking burgundy or bottle green.'

'Honestly, you wouldn't think she was a grown woman, Cassie,' Lydia grumbled to her friend. 'I feel like I'm back at school, with some other little girl trying to rule the roost and leaving me out of all the games.'

'Never mind, she'll settle down in time, I'm sure. I expect she feels a bit insecure, coming into a household as a newcomer.

Lydia wasn't so sure. She was beginning to think that Thea wouldn't rest until she had her stepdaughter banished from the household. Cassie thought that this was over-dramatising the situation.

'Poor little Cinderella,' she teased. 'Think yourself lucky that you don't have any ugly stepsisters! Perhaps you should go away for a bit. Don't you have any doting aunts you can go and stay with?'

But Lydia had nobody to turn to. Her mother had been an only child, and all her father's people were back in Scotland, as he had emigrated to Canada alone as a young man, determined to make his fortune. Whatever needed to be done to resolve the situation was in her hands alone.

Another shock awaited her. Apart from mealtimes, or the occasions on which she met Cassie, she had begun to spend more and more time in her bedroom, reading or sewing. One morning, Thea came into the room without knocking, and handed Lydia clippings from a newspaper. Puzzled, she glanced up at her stepmother.

'I don't understand. Why are you showing me this, Thea?'

'Surely you can see for yourself. They are advertisements for teachers, needed in the country schools. I thought you might like to apply.'

'But I'm not a teacher!'

'Don't be so feeble, girl. You've had a good education, which is being wasted here. They'll jump at the chance to hire you. Why, most of the time the teachers are girls who have only just completed their schooling themselves. Just give it some thought, all right?'

Lydia felt the tears springing from her eyes. She brushed them away angrily. She was not about to take this lying down. Her father was still at home. She would fight fire with fire. She stood up and rushed down to his study.

'What would you think about me applying for one of these positions, Papa?'

She would not say that it was all

Thea's idea, or he would freeze up at once. She handed him the clippings. He frowned.

'Have you any idea what you're asking, child? Do you know what life in a country school is like?'

'Not really, Papa.'

'Then let me set you straight. The school boards are often composed of men who have very little education themselves, and are therefore out of sympathy with what the teacher tries to do. In return for a pittance, you would be the sole instructor in a small, badly-heated building, out in the middle of nowhere, in which you could be asked to teach as many as fifty children, of all grades. So you really think that you could keep the children in order under such circumstances?'

Lydia shook her head in silence, as he went on.

'And see what it says here.'

He stabbed a finger at the print.

'Board round. I suppose you know what that means?'

'No, Papa.'

'I thought not. It means that one family would offer you board and lodging for a week or so, before handing you on to the next family. You would be required to live in as a member of each family, possibly in deplorable conditions, with absolutely no redress if things went wrong. I simply cannot understand why you should wish to leave your comfortable home for such a reason. If it is what you wish, to help the poor, I can arrange for you to do some suitable charitable work right here in Kingston.'

'Yes, Papa. Are you saying that you would prefer that I don't apply for these posts?'

He snorted.

'I absolutely forbid it! Now, let us say no more about it.'

Hiding a smile, Lydia went in search of her stepmother.

'I asked Papa's permission to take work as a teacher, and he won't hear of it. In fact, I believe it annoyed him very much that I could even consider such a thing.'

Rewarded by a glare from Thea, Lydia went upstairs, feeling very much better. This was war. Round one to her. However, she very much doubted that Thea would give in so easily.

3

Lydia, her father and Thea were dining alone, and the maid had just removed the soup plates and was bringing the next course.

'Alex, I've been thinking,' Thea said.

'Yes, darling?'

Alex McFarlane was in good humour, having concluded a most successful business transaction that day.

'Now that I have had the house redecorated to my satisfaction, would it not be a good idea to hold a series of entertainments for dear Lydia's benefit?'

Lydia looked alarmed. What was coming now? She was aware that her father's eyes were upon her.

'Musical evenings, you mean, Thea?'

'Perhaps, or tea parties and so on.'

'Hardly my sort of thing,' he replied, with raised eyebrows.

'No, no, Alex. Naturally you wouldn't be expected to pour tea! However, I'm sure you'll agree that it's time that Lydia was introduced to suitable young men of her own age and social class, if she is ever to find a husband.'

He laughed.

'Surely there is plenty of time for that, my dear!'

'Lydia is almost twenty years of age, Alex. You don't want her to be left on the shelf, do you?'

'Hardly that, Thea, but if you wish to organise these entertainments, by all means do so. I'm sure that Lydia would be most grateful.'

Lydia, her face burning with embarrassment, kept her eyes on her plate. How dare they talk about her as if she wasn't present? She knew what Thea was up to! As usual, she decided to confide in Cassie.

'Another ploy to get me out of the house, of course, while pulling the wool over Papa's eyes. Of course, there's no point in speaking to him. He just wouldn't believe me.'

Cassie smiled.

'Why not let her go ahead and give these parties? She can hardly do anything without inviting our friends as well, and if she can drum up a few extra men to add to the numbers, all the better. The Royal Military College is full of them!'

Lydia had to agree that it wouldn't do any harm. After all, even Thea couldn't bring in a clergyman to marry some unknown man to Lydia while they were all listening to someone playing a sonata on the piano! She laughed at the very idea.

She wasn't laughing, however, when she overheard a conversation which proved the extent to which her stepmother was prepared to go. She had just arrived home from playing tennis with Cassie and was passing the conservatory door, when she heard her name mentioned. Of course, no lady would ever eavesdrop, but on this occasion she felt it was justified.

Thea and some man, unknown to Lydia, were hidden from her by a gigantic fern in an earthenware pot, and in her soft shoes she was able to creep closer without being detected.

'But I'm not in love with the girl,' the man was saying. 'If I'm to marry her you'd have to make it worth my while.'

'She's no great beauty, I agree,' the reply came, 'but she's been well educated and certainly knows how to run a household. You could do worse.'

Stung, Lydia missed his reply. No great beauty, indeed! Her eyes were dark, her brown hair was plentiful and glossy, and she had often been complimented on her smile. She was slender and fairly athletic and her face was nothing to be ashamed of. Unfortunately, Thea's nature was such that she couldn't help running her stepdaughter down even when she wasn't present. Thea was speaking now.

'I assure you, I can get her father to cough up a good dowry, Frederick. He's a rich man, and Lydia is his only child.'

'And what's in it for you?' the unknown Frederick sneered.

'I get rid of the irritating creature, always saying, 'Mother did it this way' or 'We've never had dinner as late as this. Cook doesn't like it and I'm afraid she'll give notice.' None of Lydia's business if she does!'

Frederick was still not convinced.

'As I told you, I'm not in love with her. I don't even know the girl.'

Thea's laugh was unpleasant.

'Do you think I'm in love with old Alexander McFarlane? It's his lifestyle I want. Now then, all you have to do is to marry Lydia, produce a couple of children, and then find yourself someone more to your liking, take a mistress, take two! Where's your imagination, man?'

Sensing that the conversation was coming to an end, Lydia tiptoed away. Once in her room, she rang the bell, and when a maid appeared, she demanded to know who Mrs McFarlane's visitor was.

'That's Mr Frederick Marshall, miss. Cook says he's a lawyer friend of madam's brother. Originally from Montreal or somewhere like that. A single gentleman, I believe.'

This latest idea of Thea's was the last straw. How could she be so evil? Lydia realised then that she had to get away. Not that she could be forced into marriage, of course, but Thea could make things most unpleasant for her stepdaughter if her plans were thwarted yet again. Lydia had done her best to accept the woman's presence in the house, and it broke her heart to think that a wedge was being driven between herself and her father.

While she had no wish to teach school, there must be something else she could do. Thanks to Thea she had the idea of looking in the **Help Wanted** section of the newspaper, and she made her way to the library to see what she could find.

She was disappointed. Mothers' helpers and hired girls to work on farms seemed to be in great demand, but she didn't fancy that work. Shop assistants were also needed, but those jobs paid very little, and she didn't see how she could support herself on those wages, her whole idea being to leave her father's house. Probably most of the young women lived at home, and contributed to household expenses there, or perhaps shared rooms in some boarding house.

In any case, it would certainly cause a rift between her and her father if his friends saw her working in a shop, which was unknown for ladies of their class. She would have to leave Kingston. Idly, she turned to the personal columns, and was struck by the number of men looking for wives, sight unseen. Huge tracts of land had opened up in the West in recent years and hordes of single men had joined the thousands of immigrant families going there as homesteaders.

For people who had owned little or nothing in the way of land in what they still called the Old Country, the idea of suddenly possessing hundreds of acres was a temptation they could not resist. In communities where there were few single women it had become the custom for men to advertise for what were known as mail order brides.

Lydia noticed one plea which struck her as promising, and excitement took hold of her. It would do no harm to respond to this advertisement. She could always back out later. Besides, it would probably come to nothing.

It sounded rather romantic. Probably these men were lonely and just needed somebody to share their lives. She could imagine herself, dressed in a frilly apron, placing a nutritious meal on the table when her husband came through the door after a day's work. She had no idea of what her own work on the farm would entail; perhaps feeding a few hens, or something? It would be nice to have fresh eggs to gather.

So she sat down to reply to the advertisement, and to her astonishment,

Joseph Dunfield's acceptance came by return of post. Still not sure of her next move, Lydia made an excuse to go to see Cassie.

'Are you mad?' Cassie shrieked. 'Utterly, completely mad?'

'You've no need to speak to me in that tone of voice,' Lydia bridled. 'I haven't made up my mind yet, anyway.'

'Even though this Joseph Dunfield is sitting out there all alone, getting ready to welcome his bride to his home? How could you, Lydia?'

'Well, naturally, I'll let him know if I decide not to go, Cassie. But I'm certainly thinking of accepting his proposal. Anything would be better than staying here under Thea's thumb.'

'That's hardly the point. What if you go all the way out there — two thousand miles, Cassie — and when you get there you don't like the man? Marriage is for life!'

Lydia shrugged.

'So it would be with any other man I might marry. Suppose I hadn't overheard

Thea and Freddie talking. He might have convinced me that he loved me, and I wouldn't have discovered it was a sham until after the wedding, when it was too late. At least this way we'd be starting out with nothing to hide.'

'Unless the man turned out to be a drunkard or something,' Cassie muttered. 'But the point is, you've been used to having servants all your life. How are you going to manage the cooking and so on?'

'We did have cooking lessons at Miss Harper's,' Lydia reminded her, referring to their former school, Miss Harper's Academy for Young Ladies.

'Invalid foods!' Cassie scoffed. 'A husband will want more than junket and coddled eggs. Stews and pies would be more like it, I imagine.'

'So I'll buy a cookery book. Any fool can follow a set of instructions.'

Cassie thought there must be more to it than that, or surely everybody would be a successful cook, but she knew from experience that it was useless to interrupt when her friend was in full flow.

She was frightened for Lydia. She could not imagine such a life. She herself wanted a beautiful wedding at St George's, after which she would settle down in Kingston with her husband, to raise a family.

'If you must get away from home, why not stay with us for a bit? I'm sure Mother wouldn't mind. That would give you time to think.'

Lydia shook her head.

'That's very kind, Cassie, but it would do no good in the long run. No, I've made up my mind. I'll go West.'

She had to get her clothes ready without alerting Thea, who would want to know why she was taking out her winter things so early. She wrapped up her beloved china ornaments carefully and some books which had belonged to her mother, and managed to transfer them to Cassie's home without being detected. She could send for them later.

After the fiasco with the bedroom curtains she didn't trust Thea not to destroy her things, or to give them to charity, especially when the house would probably be in an uproar when her disappearance was discovered. She allowed herself a grim smile as she pictured her father's wrath. She would leave him a note, of course, without saying exactly where she was going.

The thought crossed her mind to add that she was leaving because living with Thea had become impossible, but that probably wouldn't do any good. If he had had any idea at all of the way in which his new wife behaved towards his only child, he would not have allowed matters to get this far.

A week later, trembling in her boots, Lydia crept out of the house and made her way to the station. The train was a few minutes late and she was on tenterhooks, expecting to see the tall figure of her father appearing at any moment, ready to drag her home in disgrace. But she hadn't been missed, and soon she found herself sitting on a hard, wooden seat inside one of the colonist cars, waiting for the engine to get up steam.

The great adventure had begun.

4

The journey west was a nightmare. As a major shareholder in the railway company, Alexander McFarlane owned a private coach which was joined to the train whenever he wanted to go out of town. Lydia had gone with him on several of these trips in the pre-Thea days, and was used to travelling in comfort. The living compartment had deep armchairs and a solid oak table, covered with chenille and there were strategically placed lamps for when the passengers wanted to read, sew or play cards. The windows had heavy red curtains to match the tablecloth and these could shut out the night after dark.

The sleeping quarters she remembered had well-sprung beds where the traveller could recline in comfort, watching the scenery slip past. As a child, Lydia had loved to look out of the window at night as the train sped through the countryside, dotted with small houses whose lights shone out into the darkness. She imagined the lives of the people inside and made up stories about them.

In her innocence, she expected that train travel was always like this. Nothing had prepared her for conditions in the colonist car where settlers, poor people for the most part, had paid the cheapest fares to get them to their destination. The long, rickety coach was filled with hard, wooden seats with bunks tucked under the roof, and there was a pot-bellied stove at the end of the aisle on which, as she was later to learn, some of the passengers would cook their meals, filling the compartment with strange smells. Lanterns swung from the ceiling as the train rattled along.

Every available space was filled with bags and bundles, but even so, small, runny-nosed children managed to dash up and down the aisle, jostling the other passengers as they went. Squashed between a large, grey-haired woman and a foreign-looking man who reeked of garlic, Lydia wondered how she could ever manage to tolerate four or five days of this.

But the time did pass. Turning away from the man, who leered at her with tobacco-stained teeth, Lydia struck up a conversation with the older woman, who turned out to be quite friendly. She was going to visit her married daughter, who was about to have a baby, she said. When she heard that Lydia was going to be married, she clasped her hands together with excitement, asking one question after another, without waiting for an answer. She seemed to assume that the bridegroom had known Lydia in Kingston and had gone ahead to prepare a home for them.

'It's a shame you can't be married in your own church,' she went on, 'but him travelling back east would cost money, so no doubt the pair of you are doing the right thing. But, oh, your poor mother! How sad she'll be, not to see your wedding!'

Lydia explained that her mother had died some years earlier, and the woman clucked sympathetically and, fortunately, went off into a long description of her daughter's wedding, which had taken place before the couple left Toronto, where the family was from. Lydia let the talk flow over her, letting the woman assume that she had known her prospective bridegroom for some time. She had the feeling that if she let slip that she was a mail order bride she might be greeted with a frown of disapproval.

But there was nothing wrong with what she was doing, she told herself defiantly. Hundreds of women went West to be married. It was all rather romantic, really. Together with a handsome husband she would raise a family of sturdy children and help to build up this new country.

Her companion, who was called Mrs Freebody — but insisted on being called Flora — soon recognised that Lydia was in for a shock about what awaited her on the prairie. The woman's eyebrows rose higher and higher as Lydia rattled on about life on the farm. Feeding the chickens and cuddling the dear little lambs seemed to be the sum total of her knowledge of country life. She had owned a toy farm, once, a pretty house surrounded by a white picket fence. She understood that she might have to wait a while, but eventually she, too, would have such a home and life would be so wonderful.

'Are you sure you know what you're doing, dear? You're a city girl, aren't you?'

Mrs Freebody's daughter had told her about life on the prairie, about the long winter nights when the wind howled over their dwelling, and the scorching sun in summer, and the insects that plagued the settlers as they worked to clear their land. Some of those people were too poor to buy oxen or horses and many a woman was hitched to the plough as her husband tried desperately to scratch a living from the soil. Her daughter had been raised in the city, too, but her husband was a farmer's son so they had known what they were getting into.

'I expect I'll soon learn,' Lydia said cheerfully. 'I'm strong and healthy and I know I'll enjoy country life. I hated living in the city with nothing much to do all day expect going to change my library book, or discussing the latest fashion with my friend, Cassie.'

'I expect you will,' Mrs Freebody said, determined to hold her tongue.

No point in upsetting the girl when they were stuck on this train in the middle of nowhere, she thought. Let her see for herself what lies ahead, and hope she'll have the sense to turn tail and go home if it doesn't suit her. That's if she has the money to do so, of course. If she hasn't, well, like many another, she's made her bed and will have to lie on it.

Mrs Freebody turned her head aside and fell into a doze.

They reached Cold Creek at last, just as the sun was going down. Lydia staggered off the train, dragging her valise behind her. She looked around with interest, seeing a straggle of houses which bordered a wide street. The place seemed busy enough. Some folk were boarding the train, or loading goods which were obviously being shipped somewhere else.

A large group, which included several youngsters, stood about doing nothing. She was later to learn that people always gathered at the station when the evening train was due, just to see what was going on. Life was dull out here in the middle of nowhere.

Several other travellers had climbed down from the train and were being greeted by friends. Lydia watched enviously as hugs and kisses were exchanged before the new arrivals were taken off to the wagons and buggies which awaited them. Her eyes scanned the crowd anxiously as if she expected Joseph to come striding forward to claim her, but that wasn't to be.

She realised all at once that she had done something stupid. Instead of writing to let him know the day and time of her arrival, she had planned to surprise him. She was familiar with the farming country on the outskirts of Kingston, from her drives with her father, and had assumed that the terrain here would be much the same. Back home the farms tended to be one hundred acres in size, with all the houses visible from those of their neighbours, but it was all very different here, where the land stretched endlessly across the prairie and the homesteads were much bigger. She had no idea where to go, or what to do next.

Holding up her skirts to keep them from trailing in the dust, she trudged across to a nearby store, where she thought she could ask directions. Inside, the place was full from floor to ceiling with every possible item that a homesteader might want — groceries on shelves and in barrels, pots and pans, tools, bags of seed, bolts of cloth and boxes of buttons. An enormous cheese stood on the counter with a wire cutter beside it. An enticing smell of coffee came from an enamel pot on a wood stove that blasted heat into the room.

A pleasant-looking woman greeted Lydia.

'Hello, just off the train, are you?'

Lydia sank down on one of the cane chairs that had been provided for waiting customers.

'Yes, I am. I don't suppose that coffee is for sale, is it? I'd love a cup, if that's all right.'

'Not for sale, miss, but free for the asking. Take milk and sugar, do you?'

Lydia sipped gratefully, but realised that time was passing and she had to find the Dunfield place before dark.

'Um, can you direct me to the home of Mr Joseph Dunfield, please?'

'Joe Dunfield? Why, sure. He lives three miles out, towards Goose Hollow. Are you kin of his, maybe?'

Lydia gulped. She felt that woman was being too inquisitive, but it wouldn't do to put her back up by being snooty. She was sure that, living out in the wild, it was necessary to get on well with everyone, for who knew when she might need their friendship?

'I'm here to marry Mr Dunfield,' she said, her heart sinking when she saw the woman's jaw drop.

'Oh, but, my dear, you can't do that!'

'I don't see why not,' Lydia said stiffly. 'It's all quite above board. We've corresponded and he's expecting me.'

Whatever answer the woman might have given was lost when the door opened and a man strode in. He was tall, at least six feet, and sun-bronzed. Lydia noted that he needed a haircut, but the too-long black curls were certainly appealing. He gazed at her out of dark eyes, and she experienced a sudden frisson of attraction which caused her to lower her eyes in confusion. Could this be her intended bridegroom? For one wild moment she imagined herself in his arms.

'This young lady is looking for Joe Dunfield.'

Lydia intercepted a meaningful look which the woman directed at the newcomer. She was startled to see that his jaw dropped as well. Just what was wrong with Dunfield if both of them seemed so alarmed?

'Oh, you can't go out there,' the man told her.

Lydia lifted her chin and said firmly, 'I certainly can! I've come all this way to marry Mr Dunfield, and I have no intention of letting him down now. All I need is for someone to give me directions to his farm, and I'll be on my way.'

'Seems like you'd better take the lady out there, Travis Brown!'

The woman had a cold look in her eyes now.

'Come on, Frances, you can't saddle me with this.'

'Oh, yes, I can, young man! And you better get going before it gets dark.'

Something was going on between the two that Lydia couldn't understand, but she told herself that it wasn't her business. When it became apparent that neither Lydia or Frances was prepared to back down, Travis Brown shrugged and told Lydia to follow him outside. There, he handed her into an ancient wagon and threw her valise up behind her. Then he climbed up beside her and urged his horse into a trot.

Jostled from side to side as the wagon lurched along the rough road, Lydia looked up at the silent man sitting beside her. It all seemed very strange, but she was on her way at last.

5

Travis Brown seemed to have little to say. Lydia made several attempts at conversation but when her overtures were met with grunts or one-word answers, she lapsed into silence. The wagon rattled from side to side over the rutted road and she longed to reach her destination and settle down to a good meal. She was so hungry that she remembered with longing the simple food she had eaten on the train.

Passengers had been expected to provide and cook their own food, something which Lydia had failed to take into account, but she hadn't gone hungry. At every stop the train was boarded by enterprising housewives carrying baskets laden with homemade items which they hoped to sell. There was seldom anything left when these women left the train, but as Lydia hadn't thought to equip herself with a frying pan or saucepan she had no means of cooking anything, so had contented herself with what she described as picnic food, sold by the local women.

'We're coming up to the Dunfield place now,' Travis said, as the wagon lurched off to the left on to a muddy track. 'You can see the house in the distance.'

Lydia looked, and gave a puzzled frown.

'Where is it, Mr Brown? I don't see it.'

Travis hid a wry smile. He had expected this.

'Straight ahead. You can't miss it. It's the only place for miles around.'

She gasped. 'That . . . that hovel? Tell me you're joking!'

'It's no joke, Miss McFarlane, and that's as good a house as you'll find in these parts.'

The building crouched low to the ground, and seemed to have grass sprouting from the walls. The only sign that people might live in it was a swirl of smoke coming from the chimney. Travis seemed to feel that some remark was called for.

'It's called a soddy,' he explained.

'A what?' Lydia felt faint.

'A soddy, a house made from earthen sods. It's the only building material in these parts. You cut turf out of the ground in chunks and use it to build walls, just like bricks. The land here hasn't been cultivated since the Ice Age went away, and the earth is filled with little roots and is tough as a board.'

Lydia made no comment and he went on.

'There are poplar trees up in the hills and those are used to make a frame for the roof, which is then covered with more sod, or earth, or anything which might keep out the rain.'

Tears welled up in her eyes as she looked up at him.

'And people are prepared to live for the rest of their lives in slums like this?'

'Not slums, Miss McFarlane,' he said gently. 'They come here from all over the world, hoping for a better life, and those who are prepared to work hard will get it, eventually. They had to live somewhere, and these places don't cost much to build. Some day they will all be gone, replaced by fine houses. Cities will spring up all across these prairies. There are golden opportunities for all. That's why they call this the Golden West.'

'I don't need a sermon, Mr Brown. All this is new to me, that's all. I'll manage to cope in due course, I expect.'

The wagon drew up in front of the house and Travis jumped off to help her down.

'Are you sure you want to do this? I'd be happy to take you back to town if you've changed your mind.'

'Quite sure, thank you! If you'll be so kind as to hand me my valise.'

As he gathered up the reins, he looked at her for a long moment.

50

'I'll come by in the morning, Miss McFarlane, and see what you want to do.'

'That won't be necessary, thank you.'

'I'll come anyway.'

He drove the wagon round in a wide circle and left. Lydia watched him until he was just a dot on the horizon, and then she took a deep breath and marched towards the house. There was one tiny window, but she thought it might be rude to peer inside, so she went up to the door which was made from unpainted planks. She knocked firmly and was surprised when a baby began to wail inside.

The door was flung open by a harassed-looking young woman who snapped, 'For goodness' sake, did you have to make such a racket? I've only just got Jabez settled and now he's wide awake again!'

She stopped when she saw Lydia.

'Sorry, I thought you were my husband. My baby is teething and he's almost driven me mad these past few days. Can I help you at all?'

A dirty-faced toddler now appeared from inside and clung to his mother's skirts, sucking his thumb.

'Get back inside, Zachariah! You'd better come in as well, miss. We're letting the mosquitoes in.'

Lydia ducked her head to avoid hitting it on the low doorframe. The interior of the house was gloomy, and cluttered with all sorts of household goods. A blanket was strung from the ceiling on a sagging rope and behind it Lydia glimpsed a bed, covered with a jumble of quilts. The best piece of furniture in the place was a hand-carved, four-poster cradle on rockers, in which the howling Jabez was installed. Silently, the toddler took hold of one of the posts and began to rock. The noise stopped.

'Sit down, why don't you?'

The woman swept a pile of garments off one of the wooden chairs, and signed to Lydia to sit down. Lydia wondered who she was. A neighbour, coming to make the house ready to welcome its new mistress? Not a maid, surely, with those two little boys.

'I'm Lydia McFarlane,' she said. 'I expect Mr Dunfield has told you about me.'

The woman shook her head.

'I haven't come to the wrong place, have I? This is Mr Dunfield's house, Mr Joseph Dunfield?'

'Yes, yes, it is.'

'But he's not here at the moment, I see.'

Lydia peered around as if she expected to see him jumping out from behind the blanket.

'He's out working. What is this all about, Miss McFarlane?'

'I've come out here to marry Mr Dunfield. I thought he might have been expecting me, though I didn't say which day I'd be arriving.'

The woman sat down heavily on the one remaining chair.

'I don't understand. I'm Rose Dunfield, Joseph's wife.'

Anger welled up in Lydia when she realised she'd been duped.

'You mean he's been writing me flowery letters, telling me how he wants me to come and be his wife, and he's married already!'

The tears began to roll down her face. She despised herself for being so weak, but she was hungry and exhausted, and had come so far, and now everything had fallen apart. Rose Dunfield looked at her sympathetically.

'What you need is a good cup of tea! The water is just on the boil, and I daresay you could use something to eat, as well. I won't serve supper until Joseph comes in, but I have new bread of today's baking, and apple jelly, if that will suit you.'

Lydia nodded gratefully as Rose went on.

'And when you've got that inside you, you can tell me how all this came about!'

Fortified by the simple meal, Lydia told her story, how she had answered

54

the advertisement for a mail order bride and had received a fine letter in return, inviting her to come to the Cold Creek district to be married.

'Couldn't be Joe as wrote that letter,' Rose said. 'He can just about sign his name, that's all. Mind you, he could have got somebody else to write it for him. He was a bachelor until a week ago, when I married him. My man died back in the winter, leaving me on my own with them two. I couldn't manage on my own, and Joseph needed a wife, so we figured we might as well team up. This is no place for a man or a woman on their own. That's why the papers back East carry all those ads like you saw, from men wanting wives.'

'Is there another Joseph Dunfield in the area?'

Rose looked doubtful.

'I don't think so, unless Joe has cousins. I don't know that much about his family yet. But you can ask him yourself. I hear him coming now.'

Lydia braced herself to meet the man

she had expected to marry. He came into the house, peeling off his coat to reveal dirty overalls.

'Supper ready, Rose? I could eat a horse!'

He was a short, wiry man with a jagged scar down one side of his face. His hair appeared to have been cut by someone who had put a pudding basin on his head and clipped round the edges. Lydia noticed with distaste that his fingernails were black with dirt, and chided herself for being snobbish. A man could hardly work the land without getting a bit grubby!

'We've got a visitor, Joe,' Rose stated.

He grunted.

'So I see. Can't you keep them brats quiet?'

The baby had begun to grizzle again and Rose bent over the cradle to pick him up. She was obviously no down-trodden wife for she faced her husband squarely and told him to sit down.

'I've got a bone to pick with you, Joe Dunfield!'

'Oh, aye? And what would that be?'

'This is Miss McFarlane. She's come from back East to marry you, she says.'

He threw back his head and laughed.

'Left it a bit late, then, hasn't she? Did you think I was one of them Mormons, missy, them as has more than one wife?'

'That was in the old days. They don't do that no more. This lady answered an ad in the paper and got a letter signed Joe Dunfield, Cold Creek, telling her to come ahead here.'

'Well, it weren't me,' he said, losing interest.

'I guess you'll have to turn tail and go back where you come from,' Rose told Lydia. 'You'll have to stay here tonight, of course. You can't go walking back to town in the dark. You're welcome to share what we have, and if you're not too fussy to bed down on a pile of hay, you can sleep on the floor.'

She seemed confident that her husband was not responsible for Lydia's plight, and was not prepared to waste time trying to get to the bottom of it. That night, Lydia tossed and turned on her prickly bed and remembered Travis Brown's promise to return in the morning. She hoped that he was a man of his word.

6

Frances Helferty gestured to Lydia to sit down. There was nobody in the store and she seemed glad of the company.

'You knew that Mr Dunfield was married, didn't you!' Lydia asked.

'That I did,' the older woman agreed.

'Then why didn't you tell me,' Lydia wailed, 'instead of letting me go all the way out there? I've never been so embarrassed in all my life!'

'And would you have believed me, child? I thought it best to let you go out there and see for yourself. I knew that the young fellow would bring you back here. He's a good man, is Travis Brown. So what will you do now? Go back East?'

Lydia tilted her chin up bravely.

'No, I won't! I've come all this way, and I'm here to stay. Rose Dunfield agrees with me. She says there are hordes of bachelors in these parts, all in need of wives. I can afford to take my pick!'

Mrs Helferty grinned.

'That's my girl! But what do you plan to do while you look around?'

'I don't have much money, so I suppose I'll have to find a job. And I'll need a place to stay. Are there boarding houses round here?'

'Josephine Drury lets rooms, though mostly to travelling salesmen. She might put you up if you ask her nicely, but before you decide, why don't you stay here with me?'

Lydia had taken an instant liking to the voluble Irishwoman, but Mrs Helferty kept a store, not a boarding house.

'Yes, with me. I'm not as young as I used to be, and some mornings my rheumatics are so bad I can hardly roll out of bed. A young thing like you, you ought to be able to get up early in the morning, and you could take charge in here. It's never very busy until the trains come in, anyway. Business isn't all that brisk so I can't pay much, but there's a spare room upstairs and you could have that as part of the bargain.'

Lydia's eyes lit up. Only a few hours earlier her prospects had seemed bleak, but now she had a roof over her head and a job, and she wasn't likely to go hungry in a store which stocked all kinds of food!

'Not only that,' Mrs Helferty said slyly, once the bargain was sealed, 'but if there's any place where you can meet fellows, it's right here. Sooner or later they all have to come to town for supplies, and they'll be lined up six deep once they see a pretty face behind the counter. Good for business, see.'

* * *

Their arrangement worked well. It soon transpired that Mrs Helferty was lonely. By day, she had plenty of company in the store, but in the long evenings she had been on her own, with only her

61

sewing and The Free Press Weekly to keep her busy. She was happy to tell Lydia the story of her life, and Lydia was glad to listen because the older woman had a wealth of knowledge to pass on.

'Were you a mail order bride, too?' she asked, when she eventually felt comfortable asking personal questions.

'Bless you, no. Me and my Sean kept a little shop back in Ontario, and when they started opening up the West he decided that this was the place to be. 'We'll start up a general store,' he says, 'in some little place that looks as if its ready to grow into something bigger, and we'll make our fortune.' Of course, the streets weren't paved with gold, we soon found that out, but we worked hard and had a good enough life. My only sorrow was that we'd hoped for a big family, but the children didn't come. Well, my Sean died a few years back, leaving me on my own.'

She sighed, turning to pick up a framed photo of a bearded man which stood on the heavy sideboard.

'I wonder you didn't remarry, if there are as many lonesome bachelors around as you say.' Lydia smiled.

'Huh! I know when I'm well off! Farming is not for me, and it's just as well I recognised that fact when I did, for a farm wife needs to be strong as an ox, and look at me now, all crippled up with rheumatism. Oh, there was one who came a-courting but I could see he just wanted to get his feet under the table in a snug little business! I soon sent the miserable little weasel packing.'

Mrs Helferty was quite right. When word got around that an unattached girl was serving in the store, the young men flocked to meet her. Lydia was greeted with shy looks from bashful lads, bold remarks from some who should have known better, and some unintelligible words from a handsome man who only spoke Danish.

Despite all the attention, she found herself always waiting for Travis Brown to appear, and on the rare occasions when he did come to town she felt herself going weak at the knees. Unfortunately, he gave no sign of being similarly attracted to her, simply picking up the supplies he needed and giving her a curt nod as he plunked his money down on the counter before striding off.

'He's not married, is he, Mrs Helferty?'

'Travis? Oh, no, he's not married,' Frances replied quietly.

It seemed to Lydia that the older woman might have said more, but all she did was to get up and fold her apron before limping upstairs.

Travis was evidently something of a mystery man, and Lydia was determined to find out more about him. Her opportunity came when she went to church one Sunday and the minister announced that a house-raising was to be held at a nearby homestead the following Saturday. Frances explained that on such occasions all the women gathered together to provide food for the men, and a good time was had by all. Women enjoyed a good gossip, children raced around playing, and in the evening everyone relaxed and there was dancing and music out of doors.

'I suppose they're going to put up another of those wretched huts,' Lydia said, wrinkling her nose. 'Those soddies, as they call them. Horrid name!'

'No, as it happens it'll be a frame house, on the edge of town here. A car load of lumber is coming in on tomorrow's train. The house is for the Armbrusters. They've put in their time living in one of those wretched huts as you call them, and now they'll move on to something better.'

Lydia blushed. Mrs Helferty probably thought she was being snooty, but honestly, even calling this a town was stretching it; a few primitive streets with a saloon, a handful of houses and this store! Mrs Helferty seemed to read her mind.

'Where there is no vision the people perish,' she remarked, which Lydia knew to be a verse from the Bible.

Then Mrs Helferty relented, and asked Lydia what she intended to take to the bee, the name given to any event where people came together to work, whether it was building a barn or sewing a quilt.

'I don't know, Mrs Helferty. What would you suggest?'

'How about potato salad? That's always popular. We've plenty of potatoes on hand and you can make it in one of them new enamel wash basins we just got in, real pretty with the red rim. All the women will want one like it, so you can kill two birds with one stone.'

Lydia could just imagine the expression on the face of their cook at home if anyone suggested serving up food in a wash basin! However, it was probably a practical idea for an outdoor event.

'But I can't make potato salad, Mrs Helferty. I don't know how.'

Her employer threw up her hands in disbelief.

'You don't know how! Why, there's nothing to it at all. You just boil potatoes and throw in a few bits and pieces!'

She peered at Lydia over the top of her spectacles.

'You do know how to boil potatoes, I suppose?'

Lydia's silence said it all.

'Well, I declare! I can see I'll have to take you in hand, my girl! No farmer can afford a wife who doesn't know how to cook. Why, your husband, when you get one, he'll be out working from dawn until dusk, and he'll expect good, hearty meals. Then, when the threshers come at harvest time, you'll have to cook huge meals three times a day to feed the men. I've seen them polish off ten berry pies, all in one sitting.

'Oh, the neighbourhood women may come over to help, but then you'll be expected to do the same for them. And apart from all that, you'll need to bake your own bread and make your own preserves, salt down beans and put up meat in brine. Country women have neither the time nor the money to be running into town every day to buy supplies.'

'I'd be grateful if you'd teach me, Mrs Helferty. You're right, I'd make a useless wife. I don't know what I was thinking.'

'No need to look so down, child. You're off to a good start already, you being Canadian-born. You know what our winters are like for one thing, not like those poor souls straight out from England. There was a couple here last year, who had no idea at all. They'd come from some town in the Midlands, all thrilled at the idea of getting one hundred and sixty acres of land for ten dollars. They came expecting to find an elegant house set in beautiful parkland, not a piece of empty prairie with blizzards howling over it, and don't go calling them stupid, mind, because there's many a person coming here with the same expectations.'

Like me, Lydia thought, somehow

cheered to learn that she wasn't the only one with silly ideas.

'I'll teach you to cook. You'll never be younger to learn.'

Mrs Helferty hauled herself to her feet and made for the kitchen.

'Grab an apron and we'll get started. It's too late in the day to start a batch of bread, so we'll do pastry. You can make an apple pie, and we'll have it for supper.'

'Shouldn't we start the potato salad?'

'No, no. You can do that the morning of the bee. There's really nothing to it. I'll stand over you while you make it.'

So, on the day of the house-raising, Lydia walked to the edge of town, proudly carrying her pan of potato salad. She was made welcome by the other women and shown where to leave the food, on a trestle table set up for the purpose. Nearby, someone had made a makeshift fireplace on the ground and tin coffee pots were already bubbling merrily over the fire.

'Smells good,' a passing man remarked.

'I hope you put plenty of eggshells in there. Nothing like eggshells for making a good cup of coffee!'

Lydia wished that she was an artist, so she could paint this scene. A number of wagons were drawn up, all in a row, and the horses which had drawn them here, or in one case a team of oxen, were placidly cropping grass in a nearby paddock.

Work had already begun on the new house and the frame was up on a foundation which had been prepared ahead of time. Men were swarming all over the building and the sound of hammers and hand saws made a pleasant backdrop to the shrill cries of children who were racing about, having a fine time.

Lydia's heart skipped a beat when she noticed Travis Brown up on the roof tree, hammering away. Would he speak to her when they stopped at noon for luncheon, or dinner, as they called it here?

She felt her face grow hot as Joseph

Dunfield crossed her field of vision. Then Rose was at her elbow, carrying Baby Jabez who, mercifully, had stopped screaming.

'I see you decided to stay, then, Miss McFarlane,' Rose said to her.

'Yes, I have. Frances Helferty has given me a job in the store, and a room, as well.'

'So I heard.'

'How are you getting along, Mrs Dunfield? Is your little boy any better?'

'He's fine since the tooth came through. And me and Joe are getting on fine as well. I guess you're glad you didn't have to marry him after all, eh?'

Lydia didn't know how to reply to that. She could hardly say that once having set eyes on the man she wouldn't have touched him with a ten-foot pole! But Rose didn't seem to expect an answer, and instead was looking up at Travis Brown.

'I guess he's more your style, eh? I wouldn't have minded him myself, but he never offered. Oh, well, that's life.'

By the end of the day a very respectable-looking house stood where before there had been nothing but empty space. Lydia followed the other women inside, listening to their murmurs of approval. Before the night was out there would be quite a few husbands harried by wives who demanded to know when it would be their turn to have such a home.

The fortunate owner of the new dwelling looked about her with shining eyes, talking about the wallpaper she would have one day and the furniture which would be hers in the future. Perhaps even a piano! But she knew that would all have to wait. For the moment, though, her heart was full.

When the last crumb of food had been eaten, and the sun had set over the prairie, the fiddles were tuned up and the dancing began with the waltzes and mazurkas when everyone jiggled and twisted in time to the music, and a good time was had by all.

Far from being a wallflower, Lydia

found herself in great demand. One young bachelor after another came to claim her, even the Dane, who had no words of English except, 'Please.' Then she was swept into Travis Brown's arms, and she felt as if she had belonged there for ever.

When their dance was over, he didn't return her to the benches where the other women sat waiting, but kept her standing until the fiddlers began a new tune, and then they danced on, until it was time for the musicians to take a break to quench their thirst. A young, black-haired Irish boy was propelled forwards by his friends, and told to sing. His pure voice soared upwards, bringing tears to the eyes of the older women.

In the gloom, Lydia felt Travis's arms tighten around her, and she found herself raising her face to receive his sweet kiss. In that moment she knew that she wanted to spend the rest of her life with him, but when the evening was over, he did not ask to see her home, but drove off into the darkness, leaving her to walk home with the rest of the town crowd.

Hurt and bewildered, she wondered if he had found her ready response too bold.

7

Every time the shop doorbell clanged, Lydia looked up, expecting to hear Travis Brown's firm tread on the uneven floorboards. But days passed and he didn't come. Another bachelor, Frank Pender, invited her to go driving after church on Sunday and after some hesitation she agreed. She certainly wasn't going to sit around waiting for someone who couldn't be bothered to come and explain himself to her.

She still wondered why Travis had left so abruptly. It was traditional for a girl to be escorted home by the man who had asked her for the last dance, not that Travis had asked, as such, he had simply held her in the safety of his arms until the fiddlers struck up a new tune, giving her no choice! And then he had kissed her, and what was that supposed to mean? Did he think she was a flirt, to be played with fast and loose in that way?

As it happened, she wasn't present the next time he did come to the store. Because it was a quiet time, Frances had sent her back to the parlour, urging her to take some time off. Lydia had gone happily enough. She had purchased some material to make a new blouse and was eager to cut out the pieces. The fabric was part of a number of bolts of cotton which had come in on the train the day before and the patterns were absolutely lovely.

The one she had chosen was sprigged with tiny pink roses on a pale green background which would go well with her navy blue skirt. She had lingered over a dark green tartan, but Frances had advised against it because of the difficulty of matching the checks at the seams.

'It won't sell, either,' she announced, shaking her grey head. 'Too expensive, you see, people having to buy extra on account of that. Women hereabouts don't have money to throw away.'

So Lydia was in the parlour, bent over her task and humming gently, all unaware that the man she adored was even now climbing the wooden steps to the front door.

'Hello, stranger!' Frances smiled. 'Haven't seen you for a while.'

'I've been busy,' Travis mumbled, 'and I wouldn't be here now if it wasn't that I need a new axe handle. Mine broke when I was chopping kindling.'

'Over there, by the butter churns.'

He picked up a number of the wooden handles, squinting along their length until he found one that satisfied him. Then he put his money down on the counter and turned to leave.

'In a hurry, are you? Just you come back here, young man. I've something to say.'

Reluctantly, he stopped at the door and waited while Frances hobbled around the end of the counter and came to face him.

'That girl is eating her heart out,

wondering when she's going to see you again. What's the matter with you, boy? Shy, all of a sudden, are you?'

'What girl is that?'

'Don't play games with me, Travis Brown! You know very well what girl. My Lydia. She thought there was something between the two of you, the way you danced with her so often at the bee, and if I know anything about men, you probably kissed her in the moonlight as well, eh?'

His face reddened.

'So what? I wasn't the only one who danced with her. That's what dances are for. It doesn't mean you're hooked up for life.'

She glared at him.

'You're not sweet on her, then, eh? Is that what you're trying to tell me? Listen to me, Travis Brown! This district is full of young bachelors looking for a wife, and Lydia is as sweet and pretty as they come. If you don't get a move on, she'll slip through your fingers, and you'll spend the rest of your life regretting it. Take it from one who knows.'

'All right, so I'm sweet on the girl. But nothing can come of it, so the sooner we both move on, the better. Love doesn't make a farmer's wife. She's a city girl, Fran. If a man is going to make it out here, he needs a wife who can work alongside him, and doing a lot more besides. Keeping a vegetable garden, milking the cows, making butter. Can you see Lydia doing any of that?'

'She can learn,' Frances pleaded. 'I'm teaching her to cook, Travis. She's a dab hand at making pie already.'

'It's not only that. She's used to better things than I can give her. Have you seen her clothes? Handmade boots and a fine-quality coat. Those things don't grow on trees. And you can bet she comes from some fancy house with servants. All I have is a sod house, and don't tell me she could learn to love that as well. I saw her face when I took her out to Joe Dunfield's. She called it a

79

hovel, Fran, and she was right. Nope, I'll have to look around until I find some hard-working country gal, and the best thing Lydia can do is high tail it back to the city and marry one of her own kind.'

He rushed out of the store, letting the door slam behind him. Frances sighed. She was so sure that the two were made for each other, but perhaps Travis was right. It was a hard life out here. Would love fade when the babies came and the loneliness set in on winter nights, and the crops were destroyed by grasshoppers? In her long life, Frances had seen it all. Yet she had grown fond of Lydia and wanted her to be happy. She hated the thought of the girl going back east. It would be nice if she settled somewhere nearby and produced a family of youngsters who would treat Frances like the grandmother she could never be.

'Did I hear someone in here, Mrs Helferty?'

Lydia had come in from the parlour

in search of a packet of pins.

'Just some fool looking for a new axe handle,' Frances retorted, and Lydia left the room, disappointed.

★ ★ ★

'I am not going to that box social!' Lydia snapped.

'You are so!'

The two women faced each other. Since the night of the dance, Lydia had refused to go anywhere other than to church, and even then she scurried back to the store after the service instead of standing outside chatting, as the other women did.

The box social was a popular way of raising a little money for church funds. Each unattached girl packed a delicious meal in a prettily decorated box or basket, and took it to the church hall on Saturday night. The minister held up each offering in turn, inviting the men to bid on it. The winner had the privilege of sitting with the young woman who had prepared it, and of course shared her supper.

'You know what they say about the way to a man's heart,' Frances said. 'Many a marriage has resulted from a box social, I can tell you. If it's your cooking you're worried about, I'll help you with that. It's about time you learned to make a batch of fried chicken.'

'It's all a put-up job, Mrs Helferty. We had box socials in Kingston, too, you know! The boxes are supposed to be anonymous, but everybody makes sure that they get to sit with the right person, or if they don't, it's so humiliating to stand there hoping that somebody bids on your box. What if mine was left over at the end and the minister had to come forward and pretend he was hoping to eat with me all along? I've seen that happen more than once.'

'Do you want the whole town talking about you and laughing behind their hands?'

Lydia looked at Frances in surprise.

'No, of course not. That's exactly my point.'

'And my point is that everyone knows about you and Travis Brown, so the best thing you can do is go there and face up to them, like nothing has happened.'

'There is nothing to know about me and Travis Brown,' Lydia said between gritted teeth.

'If you can say that, my girl, you don't know how things are in a small town! There's nothing that interests folks more than births, marriages and deaths. You two made an exhibition of yourselves at the bee. You're both nice, young, unattached people. Of course people are going to take an interest in you. Why, I've had more than one woman asking me when the wedding is to be.'

Lydia gave a cry of exasperation and hurried from the room. Sitting on her bed, with her face in her hands, she came to a decision. She'd show these people! So what if Travis didn't care about her? She'd go to the stupid box social and take her chances with the rest. Probably Travis wouldn't show up at all and when she spent the evening with another man, that would give them all something else to talk about.

A little voice in her head said, 'And what if he does come, and bids on someone else's box? What will you do then, Lydia McFarlane?' But she brushed the thought aside and stood up to go back to the parlour. She had to finish her new blouse, so she'd have something pretty to wear, to build her confidence.

Frances nodded placidly when she heard Lydia's decision. What next? Should she send a message to Travis, urging him to attend the social and make things right with Lydia, or would that frighten him off? Her head filled with possibilities, she spent the rest of the evening in pleasurable anticipation, trying to work out how she could bring the lovers together.

By the time the clocks struck ten she had reached a point in her dream where Travis and Lydia had brought their first child to the church to be christened, naming it after her. Not if it was a boy, of course, but Francis would do just as well!

8

The next day's train brought a shock for Lydia. Fortunately she was not in the store when the train came in. Frances had asked her to deliver an order of groceries to a neighbour who had sprained her ankle and couldn't get out to do her own shopping. The minister had dropped off her list but was unable to stay while Frances packed the items because he had other people to visit.

Lydia was glad of the chance to get out into the sunshine and mulled over the idea if, in time, they could start up a delivery service to people in the outlying districts. Of course, they would need a horse and wagon if they were to do that. Back in Kingston, the boys employed by various shopkeepers sped about on bicycles which had built-in carriers. She smiled at the notion of herself bumping and lurching over the prairie on a sit-up-and-beg machine. That certainly would start the gossips talking! Ladies did not ride bicycles!

It was lucky that the store was empty when the conductor walked in, carrying the mailbag and brandishing a poster.

'Put this up somewhere, will you, Frances?'

She knew the man well. He was a regular on the train which piled the small branch line. He was always in and out of the store, delivering goods which were too heavy for her to manage. His predecessor was not so easy-going and she had been forced to get a boy with a handcart to ferry the things in, even though they were not far from the station.

'What is it, Bert? An advertisement for something?'

'Wanted, dead or alive,' he joked.

Posters warning people of criminals on the loose sometimes flooded the countryside. Not that there were many murders out here, but there were plenty of con men, embezzlers or bigamists.

'Some bigwig back East put this one out. A missing girl. I guess she's eloped or something. Pretty girl, too.'

Alarm bells sounded in Frances Helferty's mind. She accepted the poster, taking care to seem unconcerned. When he had downed two cups of coffee and an apple turnover, made by Lydia, as it happened, he went back to the train, whistling. Only then did Frances look down at the poster, to see Lydia's face staring up at her. It had been reproduced from a studio portrait, obviously taken some years ago to judge by the hat, which was no longer in fashion, but it was easily recognisable as Lydia.

Nobody must see this until she decided what it was best to do. She crumpled it between her two hands and lifted the plate on the wood stove, meaning to burn it, but at the last second she changed her mind and smoothed it out before placing it in the pocket of her apron.

There it stayed until evening, when the supper dishes had been washed and put away, and she and Lydia were sitting in the light of the kerosene lamp, sewing. Frances cleared her throat.

'Lydia, child, something happened today which will come as a shock to you.'

Lydia looked up, her eyes wide.

'Has something happened to Travis? Please, Mrs Helferty, don't tell me he's got himself engaged to somebody else.'

'No, no, nothing like that, but this may be worse, in a way.'

She reached into her pocket and brought out the wrinkled poster and handed it over. Lydia dropped her sewing with a little cry of protest.

'It's Father! He's found out where I am and he's going to come and drag me home in disgrace. I won't go, Mrs Helferty! I just won't go! I haven't done anything wrong.'

'Calm down, child, and let's talk this through. Don't you see, the very fact that he's sending these posters out shows that he doesn't know where you are.'

'Posters!' Lydia's voice was bitter. 'He's advertised for me like a criminal, or . . . or a lost dog!'

'I expect he loves you, and wants to make sure you're all right. Any father worth his salt would want to do the same.'

'Not my father! He's treating me just like a possession!'

Even as she said it, Lydia had the guilty feeling that this was going too far. Yes, Alexander McFarlane was a strict father who liked to think his word was law, but he wasn't cruel.

True, her nose had been put out of joint when he married Thea, but he was still a relatively young man and, as he had explained at the time, he didn't want to spend the rest of his life alone. Now that Lydia was a little older, and in love for the first time, she understood what he had meant by that.

'You've never explained what you told your father when you were leaving,'

Frances went on. 'I assume you told him something. It would have been too cruel to just disappear, leaving him to wonder if you'd been kidnapped, or fallen into Lake Ontario or something.'

'I left a note,' Lydia muttered.

'Well, come on. What did it say?'

'Nothing, really. I just said I was going away, and he mustn't worry about me.'

Frances raised her eyes to the ceiling.

'And I suppose you haven't written to him since, to let him know that you're still alive?'

'How could I? The postmark would tell him where I am. Anyway,' she went on, in a small voice, 'I thought he'd disown me, so there was no point in writing.'

'Evidently he hasn't done that. So now what do you plan to do?'

'Destroy this, for a start!'

Lydia tore the poster into tiny pieces and stuffed them in her pocket.

'I don't know how that's going to help. There must be hundreds of these things scattered all over the country, pasted up in every store from here to the coast. All it needs is for some local person to take a trip away from home and you'll be recognised in an instant. Everyone knows you from working here.'

'Perhaps no-one will, take a trip, I mean.'

Frances had a look of pity on her face.

'It costs five cents to take a ride to the next station down the line. Plenty of people have friends or relatives in other places. They're always hopping on the train to attend funerals and such. That poster doesn't say anything at all about a reward being offered, but that won't stop people hoping. Once word gets out, your father will be flooded with letters from folks hoping to cash in.'

Frances was silent for a while. Then a thought struck her.

'I wonder why he thinks you might have come West. I mean, you could be anywhere by now. If I lived in Kingston

92

and had a daughter who wanted to disappear, Toronto is the first place I'd go to start looking. A big city, on the main railway line. Wouldn't that thought occur to him?'

'He's probably done that, too,' Lydia said dismally. 'He's got a lot of shares in the railways so he'd have no trouble getting the staff to distribute these things. And I imagine the first thing he'd do was to call on my friend, Cassie, to see if she knew anything. He'd worm it out of her in no time.'

'Does this Cassie know where you are, then?'

'I didn't tell her where I was coming, but she knows I was heading West as a mail order bride, and she knows I was supposed to marry a Joseph Dunfield. I know my father, Mrs Helferty. If he doesn't get results from these posters, he'll hire a private detective to track down Joseph Dunfield, and then I'll be sunk.'

'Yes, I can see that, child.'

'So I'll just have to move on, and go

where he won't find me.'

Frances leaned over and patted Lydia on the knee.

'Don't be silly, you've nowhere to go, and no money to do it with, and as soon as you got on the train you'd be spotted by someone who'd seen these posters. What is the point of running away, leaving the love of your life behind you? And if it doesn't work out between you and Travis, perhaps it would be just as well for you to go back home and settle down.'

'Never!'

Lydia knew that her life might as well be over if she consented to return to Kingston. She would never hear the last of it from Thea and her father, especially Thea, and Cassie would probably be forbidden to see her again. If she went home with her reputation in tatters, she was unlikely to make a good marriage, even if the day came when she was able to forget Travis's handsome face and feel able to begin life with somebody else.

'I shall just stay here,' she said, sounding braver than she actually felt. 'If my father finds me, I'll just face up to him and say I won't go home. He can't drag me on to the train, kicking and screaming, can he? And even if he does disown me, I don't suppose Thea will mind. She might even take my side if she thinks there's a danger of having me in the house again.'

'Why not write to her and ask her to intervene? If your father is as besotted with her as you seem to think, he might listen to her.'

Lydia shook her head.

'I know my father, Mrs Helferty. Just as he refused to hear a word against her when I tried to make him see my point of view, so he would refuse to hear anything she might say that didn't fit in with his plans for me. At least,' she added doubtfully, 'that's what I think. Of course, he might be so angry by now that he'd behave in ways I wouldn't expect.'

Frances didn't reply to this, but all

the while her mind was ticking over furiously. The only safe way for Lydia to thwart her father was to get married before he tracked her down, and that meant bringing Travis to the point! Lydia had already indicated that she had no intention of running after him and begging, so that left Frances to do something about it. But what?

9

Lydia was tidying the shelves, carefully taking down the various items and dusting them off, before attacking the floor with a corn broom. As Frances Helferty said, nobody wanted to buy foodstuffs in a place where the dust bunnies rolled around every time someone opened the door.

She had reached the section of the store where her employer stocked mousetraps and candles and galvanised pails, when the door opened with a thud and two men she didn't know burst in. Slightly alarmed, she turned to see who they were but they appeared not to notice her, and dashed up to the counter. Preparing to do battle, Lydia took a firm hold on the shovel she had just moved aside, but her gesture wasn't needed. Frances obviously knew the two men and showed no fear at their abrupt entrance.

'Gidday, Brian, Len! Got the seven devils on your tail, have you? Or maybe it's Reverend Jenks! Your sins have found you out at last, eh?'

She cackled at her own wit but her face turned serious when she saw that the pair were not returning her banter as they usually did.

'What's up, then, boys?'

'Somebody shot Joe Dunfield,' the shorter of the two blurted out.

'Shot Joe! Did somebody telegraph for the doctor? Is he going to be all right?'

'Dead as a doornail,' his companion put in.

Frances put both hands on her chest.

'I've got to sit down, boys. Just grab a cup of coffee, why don't you, on the house, and then calm down and tell me all about it.'

Lydia poured coffee and handed over the brimming mugs. Talking together like a pair of music hall artistes the men told a frightening tale.

'It happened last night. It was

rustlers, coming after his cattle.'

'Joe heard noises and went out to see what was going on.'

'He took the shotgun with him but coming out of the light he couldn't see nothing in the dark, and they got him first.'

'Rose heard the rumpus and followed him out, but by then the two had driven the cattle off, hooting and hollering. There was nothing she could do. Joe was dead before she reached him.'

Frances recovered enough to accept the cup of milky coffee, laced with plenty of sugar, that Lydia handed her.

'What a terrible thing, and them only wed a short while. That poor Rose, fancy losing two husbands within a year. How is she going to manage now, tell me that, and her with two babes. And let's pray she's not expecting another one by now, either!'

Lydia spoke up timidly.

'How did you hear about all this?'

Two pairs of eyes swivelled in her direction.

'She harnessed up the horse and put the two kids in the wagon, and headed over to the neighbour's place,' one of the men said. 'She tried to move Joe as well but she couldn't manage it, so she just covered him with a blanket and left him there. The undertaker's got him now, waiting for the police to come and take a look at him. By rights, they shouldn't have moved anything at what they call the scene of the crime, but it may take hours, days even, before the police get here, and you can't leave a corpse just lying about in the open, can you?'

A wave of faintness came over Lydia, and she dug her nails into the palms of her hands in an effort to stay upright.

'I guess those men will be long gone by now, over the border into Montana, cattle and all,' Frances said. 'So did you want something, lads, or did you just come to let us know what happened?'

It turned out that they wanted to stock up on buckshot, which she kept under lock and key. By the time they were served and on their way, Lydia had control of her emotions, but she couldn't help thinking that, had it not been for a quirk of fate, it was she who might be wearing black for poor Joe Dunfield now.

'I do hope those lads aren't planning to do anything foolish,' Frances said, biting her lip. 'This is Canada, not the Wild West of the United States in the olden days. It's one thing to get prepared in case those rustlers come back, a farmer has to protect himself, but quite another to raise a posse to go after them. Someone is liable to get hurt.'

'Like poor Mr Dunfield. What will happen now, Mrs Helferty?'

'The police will come and investigate, but I don't suppose it will do any good, Lydia. As I said, they'll be far away by now. Why would they hang around waiting to be caught, when they know the guilty parties will be hanged?'

All day long, people from town and country alike poured into the store, eager to hear the latest news of the murder. Lydia was kept busy weighing out bags of sugar and standing on tiptoe to reach items from the highest shelves as people vied for her attention.

'Mercy me, I sure hope all this excitement soon dies down,' Frances moaned, during a temporary lull.

'It's good for business, though. I haven't stopped all morning. People who wouldn't normally drive in from the country at this time of day seem to feel they ought to do their shopping while they're here, to make the trip worthwhile.'

'And there's been a lot of time wasted, too! People standing around that stove swilling coffee when they ought to be about their business!'

Tongues started to wag again that afternoon. Shortly before the mournful sound of the train's warning signal was heard, a wagon drew up in the station yard and Rose Dunfield, heavily veiled and dressed in black, was helped down by a man Frances identified as Phil

Stedman, her neighbour. Her baby lay quietly in her arms, as if he could understand the solemnity of the occasion, but little Zachariah capered up and down in glee at the thought of riding on a real train.

When it shuddered to a halt with a squeal of brakes he ran to his mother and hid his face in her skirts, peering out in delicious terror. The conductor reached down and boosted the child up into the compartment and the young widow climbed up behind him, looking back to make sure that her carpet bag of necessary supplies wasn't being left behind.

'He's coming this way!' Frances hissed, moving back from the window so as not to be seen.

'Who is, the conductor?'

'No, no, Phil Stedman. Now we'll hear the real story!'

She pretended to be busy with a jar of humbugs as the doorbell tinkled and a burly man of about fifty years old strode in.

' 'Morning, Phil! How's it going?'

'It's not good, Fran, as I daresay you've heard. Poor old Joe kicked the bucket last night. I don't know what the world's coming to! The wife is in a rare old state, thinking them rustlers is going to come back and have a go at me.'

He was obviously shaken up and needing to talk, and the wily Frances took full advantage of that.

'Poor Rose! I heard she came over to your place when it happened. Is that right?'

'Sure is! Not much else she could do. According to her the men left right after the shooting, driving Joe's few cattle ahead of them, so she was safe enough, but very shaken up, of course.'

'Of course, she would be, poor soul,' Frances murmured. 'I was surprised to see her going away now, though, what does she plan to do?'

'Oh, she's just going up the line to Poplar Springs. She has a sister there. She'll be back for the funeral, though, but they can't hold that until the police are finished looking into things.'

'But won't the police want to interview her?' Lydia wondered.

'Sure they will, but they can do it in Poplar Springs as well as here. That local train travels so slow a turtle could out-run it. Them Mounties on horse-back can get there in no time.'

By the time the store closed that night, Frances and Lydia were exhausted.

'I don't think I could face cooking a big meal,' Frances gasped, fanning her hot face. 'Guess I'll fry up a few eggs and brew a pot of tea. All right by you?'

Lydia nodded in agreement.

'What will happen to Rose now, do you think? She won't be able to stay out there on the homestead alone, will she?'

'Well, hardly! Even supposing a lone woman was able to run a farm all by herself, there's not much she can do with two little ones to care for. Nope, I think she'll have to sell up and move on. That's if it's hers to sell.'

'What do you mean?'

'I mean, if he made a will, leaving the place to her. There's a lot of men as doesn't.'

Sorry as she was for poor Rose Dunfield, Lydia thanked her lucky stars that she herself was not in that position. She was safe here in the store with Frances Helferty, and she still hoped that something would happen to bring her and Travis together. She was not to know that a dark cloud was already hanging over her and that a far worse fate was in store for them both.

10

They've arrested Travis Brown for the murder of Joe Dunfield!' The woman who had blurted out the news stared at Lydia, her eyes bright with malice.

Frances had come around the end of the counter and was urging her young assistant to sit down. Her voice seemed to be coming from far away and when the room started to swim, Lydia was dimly aware of someone pushing her head down to her lap.

'I'm all right!' she whispered, struggling to sit up.

'Now see what you've done, Hetty Collins!' Frances snapped. 'Your mouth always did travel ahead of your brain. You could have broken the news more gently, eh?'

The grey-haired woman put her basket down on the counter with a thump.

'It's not a word of a lie, Frances Helferty. Speak the truth and shame the devil, I always say.'

'Shame yourself, more like. Now, did you want something, or you are just here to spread gossip?'

'I brought you two pats of butter, but if you don't want them I'll take them elsewhere.'

She knew that Frances depended on the butter which local housewives brought to the store to barter for other goods as, unlike many people in town, the store owner did not keep a cow.

'Just you do that, then!' Frances retorted.

They were old sparring partners and she was well aware that the only outlet for this butter was in the next town. Any profit the woman might make would be wiped out by the cost of the train fares.

'Stop it! Stop it!' Lydia shouted. 'How can you squabble over a pound of butter when a thing like this has happened? For goodness' sake, tell me the whole story before I go mad!'

Mrs Collins glanced at Frances, who responded with a tiny nod.

Frances had tried to put a spoke in the woman's wheel for Lydia's sake, even though she was longing to hear the story for herself. But if the girl said it was all right . . .

'I guess you know that Rose ran outside when Joe was shot. Well, she got a look at one of the men and she told Phil it looked mighty like Travis Brown, tall, sitting straight in the saddle, the way he does. The other fellow had a bandanna over his mouth and his hat pulled down over his eyes, so she couldn't tell who that might be.'

'Stuff and nonsense! There's plenty of men that rides like that, and how would she know, anyway? She probably only got a look at his back view and it must've been pretty dark, anyhow,' Frances explained.

'Oh, but, Fran, that's not the whole story, not by a long shot. Phil had to report that to the Mounties, of course, and they went over to Brown's place, and what do you think? Joe's cattle were right there, in his corral!'

'How do they know whom they belong to?' Lydia asked in a small voice.

Hetty swung round to face her, looking triumphant.

'Why, they had Joe's brand on them, didn't they?'

Frances looked at Lydia, reassured herself that the girl was all right, then asked, 'And Travis? Where is he now?'

'In the jail house, naturally, awaiting trial as soon as the justices come to town. He keeps saying he didn't do it, but then he would, wouldn't he? If he's found guilty, he'll hang.'

'How spiteful can you get, Hetty Collins? And where is the other fellow, might I ask? There were two men, and I imagine that only one of them pulled the trigger. Travis surely is totally innocent.'

'Then the law will still get him for rustling, no mistake about that.'

The woman bustled off, looking very

pleased with herself. Neither she nor Frances noticed that she had left her basket on the counter and when Lydia pointed this out, Frances told her to put the butter in the ice-box.

'And don't you bother running after the fool. I'll enter this up in the ledger and she can get what's due to her some other time.'

An argument followed in which Frances told Lydia to go upstairs and lie down, while Lydia retorted that she needed to keep on working. They were interrupted by the arrival of Tom Makinen, who had charge of the local jail on the few occasions when it was in use, mainly when tempers flared on a Saturday night when some people had too much to drink. The jail was a small building containing one cell and a tiny room for the use of the jail keeper. Tom lived next door in a shabby frame house.

'We've got a prisoner,' he said cheerfully. 'Guess you've already heard that. The news is all over town. He'll

111

need to be fed, so if you can do the honours, Fran, we'll settle up later.'

'Can I take the food to him?' Lydia spoke up firmly.

It was unlikely that she'd be allowed to see Travis under any other circumstances.

'I guess so,' the man agreed. 'Just so long as you don't bake him a cake with a file in it so he can get away.'

He laughed at the old joke but looked abashed when the two women favoured him with icy glares.

'Best be getting back, then,' he mumbled, and made a hasty exit.

Frances nodded her approval as Lydia set to work.

'Make some hard-boiled eggs and pack up half of that Victoria sponge you made yesterday. There's no point doing him a hot meal. It would be cold as charity by the time you walked it over there. Slice up a loaf of bread and take some of that butter Hetty Collins just brought in.'

She gave a mischievous grin.

'I'm sure she'd be pleased to know she's helping feed her favourite jail-bird!'

Lydia gave a wan smile in return. Frances meant to be kind, but did she really believe that Travis was innocent? Lydia couldn't make her out. She set off for the jailhouse, her heart thumping at the thought of seeing Travis.

'Go on in,' Tom Makinen welcomed her. 'You'll be quite safe, miss. He can't get out through them bars, tee hee.'

Lydia thought that the jailkeeper must be the one person for miles around who had no inkling of her feelings for Travis, or perhaps he did know, and assumed that she wouldn't want to have anything to do with a criminal. In that case, the man simply didn't know anything about love. Feelings cannot be turned on and off like a tap, more's the pity!

Travis didn't look up as Lydia came in. He was seated on a hard, wooden bench, with his head in his hands, the very picture of despair.

'Travis,' she said softly. 'It's me, Lydia. I've brought you some food.'

'Lydia!'

He raised his head then and she was appalled to see how pale and sad he looked. He had a day's growth of beard and when he saw her eyes on it he grimaced and ran a hand over the stubble.

'Sorry about the way I look. Hardly the thing when a lady comes calling, but you see, they won't let me have a razor in case I do something desperate. They don't call it a cut-throat for nothing, you know.'

She ignored that remark.

'How are you feeling, Travis?'

'How do you think I feel?' His tone was bitter. 'Holed up in here, accused of murder! And where are my friends and neighbours in my hour of need, eh? You'd think they'd be flocking to my aid, but no. You're the only visitor I've had.'

His eyes narrowed.

'Oh, I get it. You had to come, didn't

you? I bet Tom Makinen paid Fran to supply the prisoner with food. And when it came time to deliver it, little Lydia got the short straw.'

'That's not fair! I'm here because I wanted to come! They couldn't pay me to stay away! Now stop talking nonsense, and get some food inside you!'

She removed the towel from her basket and handed the food through the bars, watching as he wolfed it down. Not quite knowing how to comfort him, she murmured words of sympathy, saying that the trial would prove his innocence and then they could forget all this.

'The Mounties always get their man,' he mumbled, through a mouthful of bread and cheese. 'And they've got me, so they won't bother looking any further.'

'Nonsense. They'll keep looking until they find the real culprits, I know they will. I have to get back to the store now, Travis, but I'll be back later.'

Picking up her basket, she left the

jailhouse without looking back. He stood in his cell, grasping the iron bars with both hands. His eyes followed her, and then she was gone.

Her eyes misting with tears, Lydia stumbled down the street. She couldn't possibly go back to work in this state. Surely Frances would understand if she took a little time to herself. If she walked to the edge of town and back she might be able to pull herself together.

She came to a siding where unwanted rolling stock belonged to the railroad company was sometimes left for a short period. One long coach was waiting there, and she looked at it with interest. It was painted in dark maroon like the one on which she had often travelled with her father. Her eyes went down to the name written on the side, and she gave a sudden jump of fear and dismay. Arrochar!

This was indeed Alexander McFarlane's private coach. Proud of his Scottish ancestry, he had named it after the clan seat of the McFarlanes. Now it was here in a siding at Cold Creek, which could only mean one thing. Her father had somehow tracked her down and was here to drag her home.

11

Frances Helferty looked up from her work in the kitchen when the doorbell jangled. She had taken advantage of the lull to make a quick batch of jam tarts, knowing that customers always knew where to find her if she wasn't present in the store. People liked to have something sweet to go with their coffee and there had been so many more customers than usual, because of the news of Travis Brown's arrest, that yesterday's baking was already sold.

'Be with you in a minute,' she called.

She almost dropped her tray of pastries when she entered the room and saw who her customer was, a tall man, dressed in clothing the like of which was never seen in Cold Creek — an overcoat which was surely made from cashmere, with a high, starched collar and silk tie showing at the throat. Spats protected his expensive-looking shoes from dust and mud. He had removed his elegant top hat to display a fine head of hair, greying at the temples.

Frances was in no doubt as to who this fine gentleman was. Despite the fact that his patrician features were very masculine, and Lydia's face was sweetly feminine, the pair were very much alike and were obviously father and daughter.

'Can I help you?' she asked, carefully setting her tray down on the small table near the stove where the coffee pot bubbled.

Under other circumstances, she would have called him sir, but that would have made their positions unequal, and she needed to maintain some position of dignity as she was probably about to have a fight on her hands.

'I'm here to collect my daughter,' he said, speaking in well-modulated tones, 'Miss McFarlane. I believe she's been staying here in this . . . '

Words seemed to fail him as his

disdainful look swept around her homely little establishment, taking in the necessities of pioneer life which filled the shelves and barrels.

'Lydia is employed by me, yes,' Frances said, hiding a satisfied smile as she saw him wince.

How dare he waltz in here, looking down his nose at everything, she was thinking. No wonder poor little Lydia left home, if this is what she had to put up with. Well, I'll give him a run for his money, see if I don't!

Alexander McFarlane frowned. The look he turned on her would have caused a lesser woman to quake in her boots, but Frances was not about to be crushed. She stared back, clenching her fists inside the pocket of her apron.

'I'd like to speak to my daughter, please, if she's not too busy scrubbing floors or whatever she's made to do here.'

'Well, you can't. She's not here. Now, mister, you've two choices. You can either go back where you came from, or you can sit yourself down and take a cup of coffee while we discuss this calmly.'

She was afraid she might have gone too far, but a ghost of a smile crossed his lips and he pointed to the coffee pot as he sat down on one of the wicker chairs nearby. Swallowing a sigh of relief, she stepped forward to fill an enamel mug, instinctively selecting the one which had the least number of chips.

'I don't know if you have children of your own, Mrs . . . er . . . '

'Helferty. And no, I don't.'

'Mrs Helferty, then, if you did you might be able to understand my feelings. Lydia is my only child and has led a very sheltered life. It was, of course, my intention to keep her at home until such time as she married, and furthermore to see that she contracted that marriage with someone suited to her position in life.'

Pompous devil, Frances thought, but she kept her expression blank and waited for him to go on.

'You can imagine my distress when she left my house like a thief in the night, leaving a note to say that she was going to be married and that I shouldn't try to find her. As if that wasn't bad enough, I learned from her friend, Cassandra, that my daughter had answered a newspaper advertisement and intended to marry some penniless settler in the West, a man she had never met, and about whom she knew nothing!'

He bristled with indignation before continuing.

'And what about the man himself? No doubt he was aware that Lydia comes from a wealthy family, and hoped that she'd come with a fortune in her purse. Can you imagine a worse fate for a gently-reared girl?'

'Well, no, not when you put it like that,' Frances replied. 'Not that it would have come to that, of course, as the man was already married before she got here.'

Oops, she had put her foot in it now! Alexander McFarlane had risen to his feet, almost purple in the face. She hoped he wasn't about to have apoplexy.

'Do sit down, Mr McFarlane. I don't mean that Joe Dunfield, the man she thought she was to marry, meant to deceive her in any way. As far as I know, he knew nothing about Lydia, and in fact he was married only a short while, to a young widow with two little boys.'

McFarlane frowned.

'Dunfield? Is he related in any way to a Rose Dunfield?'

'Yes, that's right. She is poor Joe's wife, or widow, I should say. But how do you know Rose?'

He didn't answer, and the silence between them went on for too long, forcing her to speak.

'As far as I can make out, Lydia was duped by someone who had nothing to do with Joe at all. A man trying to make a go of it out here needs a wife, and Joe had been a bachelor longer than most. His neighbours used to tease him about it, saying if he didn't soon make up his mind they'd find one for him. I guess they got the idea of advertising for one in the papers, and Lydia saw the piece and replied to it.'

'And the tricksters took it one step too far, and wrote back telling her to come,' Lydia's father said grimly. 'When I get my hands on the fellow, whoever he is, I'll wring his neck!'

'Even so, nobody could force the girl to marry him,' Frances pointed out. 'Quite apart from the fact that Lydia arrived at his home to find another woman installed there, I don't think she would have gone through with it. She took a dislike to the fellow, and I know for a fact that she was appalled by his living conditions. She's more your daughter than you may realise, Mr McFarlane.'

'Then I don't understand why she didn't get on the next train and come home,' he muttered. 'Even if she hasn't enough money she had only to give my name to the station agent and she'd have been given everything she needed.'

Frances looked at him pityingly.

'Be your age!' she said robustly.

At that moment the door opened and Lydia walked in. Her father stepped forward and they embraced awkwardly. Frances stepped into the breech.

'Take your father into the parlour, child. I'll be right here if you need me.'

'I'm not coming home, Father!'

Alexander McFarlane looked at his defiant daughter and heaved a sigh.

'I'm sorry you feel that way, but you must see that you don't belong here. I'll take you back with me, and we'll tell people that you've been away on holiday with friends. Nobody needs to know what really happened.'

'Cassie knows.'

Lydia sniffed, dabbing her eyes with an inadequate wisp of lace handkerchief.

'Cassie will hold her tongue, if she knows what's good for her.'

He could tell from the set of Lydia's

mouth that she meant to be stubborn, and decided that perhaps gentle persuasion might be best.

'Thea was so upset when you left, dear. She feels that you must have been a little jealous when I remarried, and she assured me that she had done her very best to help you adjust to the change. She wants you to know that she means to do everything she can to be a real mother to you now.'

Pigs might fly, Lydia thought, but she wisely kept her thoughts to herself.

'That's very kind,' she said aloud, 'but I'm a grown woman and I no longer need a mother.'

'Perhaps not, my dear, but I must insist that you come home with me by the next train going East.'

Lydia looked him straight in the eye, although her stomach felt as if it was full of rampaging butterflies.

'Oh, no, Papa, I have every intention of staying here. I've met the man I want to marry, and that's an end to it.'

'I've told you what you are to do!' he

thundered, whereupon Lydia burst into tears and ran upstairs, leaving him standing dumbfounded.

'That went well,' Frances observed.

She had been hovering outside the door and now felt it was time to intervene.

'Shakespeare was quite correct,' he snapped. 'How sharper than a serpent's tooth it is to have a thankless child.'

'She's not ungrateful, Mr McFarlane, merely very young and in love for the first time. If you'll let me explain things to you, then perhaps you'll understand, even if you can't agree with her. I'm afraid that if you insist on dragging her back to Kingston you'll only drive her into the man's arms. You can't keep her locked up for ever, and trains do run in both directions, you know.'

'Very well, Mrs Helferty, I'll listen to what you have to say.'

He resumed his seat and looked at her expectantly.

She swallowed hard.

'Travis Brown is a settler out here on

the prairie, a very nice young man, at least, I thought he was.'

'What do you mean, thought? Is he disreputable in some way that Lydia knows nothing about?'

'I don't know if you've heard, but Joseph Dunfield was murdered recently. He was shot when he caught rustlers in the act of stealing his cattle, and died instantly. Travis Brown has been arrested by the Mounted Police, and is to be tried for murder when the justices arrive next week.'

'And people suspect he's guilty?'

'It looks that way. Cattle with Joe's brand on them were found in the corral on the Brown place.'

'And how much is Lydia involved with this fellow?'

'They've met once or twice, that's all, and danced together. Lydia came home with stars in her eyes, and you know the rest.'

Alexander McFarlane seemed to be staring into the distance. He remembered another beautiful young girl he'd been introduced to at a dance, long years ago, Selina Harrowsmith, the woman who had become his wife, and Lydia's mother. That had been love at first sight, and their marriage had been ideal until her premature death ended their union.

Some people fall in love gradually, over a period of time. For others, it comes instantaneously, like a bolt of lightning. If his daughter was genuinely in love, who was he to place obstacles in her way? He came to a sudden decision.

'I shall stay on until after the trial,' he announced. 'That is not to say that I approve of this relationship, of course, but if the verdict goes against him and the man is hanged, Lydia will need me. I shall be quite comfortable in my private railroad car, if you can recommend an eating place. Usually when I travel I have access to the dining car on the train, but of course that will not be available under these circumstances.'

'You'll be most welcome here,' Frances assured him, 'and I have a surprise for you. Your daughter will be making some of the meals. I've been teaching her to cook in the evenings. Nothing is more important to a farmer than the meals his wife can provide.'

'That's most kind of you, Mrs Helferty. I've regretted that the school she attended did not include such classes on the curriculum. Not that Lydia will ever need to cook, once she marries and takes her proper place in Kingston Society, but my late wife always insisted it was necessary for a lady to know about these things in order to know if her cook is behaving correctly. Servants have to be kept in check, you know, or they tend to take liberties.'

Frances raised her eyes to the ceiling. The man needed a few lessons of his own, but not in the art of cooking! She would have to see what she could do to educate him while he was staying nearby.

Lydia had returned to the parlour, seemingly more composed.

'I'm sorry, Papa. I was a little distraught.'

Her father patted her on the shoulder.

'That's quite all right, my dear. Your friend here has told me all about it. I'm prepared to stay here until we learn the outcome of the young man's trial, and I understand that you have a pleasant surprise for me.'

Lydia opened her mouth to respond and Frances, afraid of what the girl might let drop, jumped in quickly.

'I've just been telling your father how well you are doing in your cookery lessons, Lydia. He is looking forward to tasting some of the dishes you've learned to prepare. I hope you like apple pie, Mr McFarlane, and one-eyed Jack.'

'What in the name of goodness is one-eyed Jack?' he asked, but Frances smiled mysteriously.

'You'll have to wait and see, won't you?'

Alexander McFarlane sampled the

offering of food while his daughter stood by anxiously, awaiting the verdict. It was a simple meal. She had made rissoles from roast pork left over from the night before, and served these with mashed potatoes, green beans and some of Frances Helferty's homemade piccalilli pickle.

It was doubtful that Lydia's father knew what a rissole was, much less tasted one before, but his gentlemanly good manners came to the fore and he praised the tasty dish.

Recognising the fact that his daughter had duties in the store, McFarlane decided to spend much of his time in his railroad car, smoking his pipe and reading. If he observed that she slipped away to the jail from time to time, he was careful not to comment on it. Frances suspected that he was biding his time until he saw how the trial went. If Travis was found guilty there would be no reason for Lydia to stay on at Cold Creek and he could whisk her away, playing the sympathetic father.

Of course, if Travis was cleared and set free, as Frances fervently hoped, that would be a different kettle of fish. On one occasion, when Lydia was nowhere to be found, her father asked Frances what she really thought of Travis. Was he a gold digger, or just playing fast and loose with his daughter's emotions?

'In my opinion, he's a thoroughly reliable young man,' she replied loyally. 'I'd say he had his head screwed on right, too. He told me that there could never be anything between the two of them because Lydia just isn't cut out to be the wife of a prairie farmer. As you've pointed out to me, Mr McFarlane, she's a city girl, brought up amidst wealth and privilege. She may think she can handle it, but she hasn't lived here as long as I have, and I've seen it all. People come West with high falutin' ideas and when real life rears its ugly head why, they turn tail and run. They take jobs in the city, or go back where they came from. Hundreds do make a go if it, I know, and some day this will be a thriving place, filled with all the advantages a person could wish for.'

'Ah,' was all he said in return, but when the station agent called later, saying he'd run out of sugar and couldn't face either coffee or porridge without it, Frances learned that McFarlane had telegraphed several messages back East.

'Not that I was poking my nose in where it doesn't belong,' he hastened to say, 'but I have to key in the messages so I can hardly avoid knowing what's being sent, eh?'

'Of course not,' Frances assured him.

She had some idea that confidentiality was supposed to be involved, but she wasn't about to mention that, as she wanted to hear what he knew, and anyway, they'd known each other for years, the agent having been a close friend of her late husband, so she wasn't just some ordinary member of the public.

'And you wouldn't believe where all

those messages were going,' he said in a low voice, leaning across the counter the better for Frances to hear.

'Lawyers and bankers and newspaper editors, and all having to do with Travis Brown. What with young Lydia being sweet on the accused, maybe she has her father working to get him off.'

'I doubt it,' Frances said. 'He's come out here looking for her. He means to take her back to Kingston with him. You can bet your bottom dollar he doesn't want his grandchildren raised in some sod house. And anyway, he's no lawyer. He made his money in railroading.'

'All them rich fellows are in cahoots,' the station agent said. 'Same as all those members of parliament. They all know each other from going to Upper Canada College when they was boys. They all help each other when they need it. They call it the old school tie, don't they?'

'Don't ask me!'

Frances shovelled sugar from a barrel into a small blue paper bag, and weighed it on her set of scales. Satisfied, she sealed it and pushed it across the counter to him.

'And if you want something nice to go with that coffee, I've ginger nuts, fresh baked today.'

He left with his purchases, leaving Frances with much to think about.

What was McFarlane up to? She couldn't figure it out. If she didn't know better she might assume that he was attempting to help his daughter's sweetheart in some way, perhaps by locating friends or relations who would speak up for Travis, or pay some fancy lawyer for his defence.

As it was, she suspected that the man was up to something, getting prepared in case Travis did get off. Not everyone who came West to farm was honest and good. There were also a lot of ne'er-do-wells whose families in Britain or other parts of Canada wanted them out of the way. These men were paid to come out to western Canada and stay there. Some played about at being farmers; a few got into trouble. Did McFarlane hope to find out something against Travis, so that he could say to Lydia that she couldn't marry the man? He was no good, and she could thank her father that he found out in time.

And, of course, not all Canadian-born fellows were saints! Those two rustlers, for one thing. A thought struck Frances. If Travis was guilty, either of killing Joe Dunfield, or of being an accomplice of the man who pulled the trigger, where was the other man? Why hadn't the Mounties found him? Travis was an intelligent chap. If he had indeed stolen poor Joe's cattle, would he have been such a fool as to put them in his own corral for all the world to see?

Her reverie was interrupted by the arrival of Lydia, in floods of tears. She seemed to do nothing but weep these days, Frances thought, a trifle crossly, but perhaps under the circumstances it was only to be expected.

'Been to see Travis, have you?'

'Oh, Mrs Helferty, it's all so terrible! He seems to have lost hope altogether. I've told him and told him that if he's innocent, which of course he is, they'll have to let him go. He says that if I believe that, I'll believe anything. I'm right though, aren't I, Mrs Helferty?'

'I'm not so sure about that, child,' Frances said grimly.

In her view, too many people had been wrongly convicted in the past, even hanged for crimes they may not have committed. Seeing Lydia's face fall, she hastened to put things right.

'Now don't you worry. The Mounties are experienced in these matters. We have to leave it all to them. Meanwhile, your job is to visit Travis and help to keep his spirits up. Tell him you love him and you'll stand by him, no matter what.'

And heaven help me if Alexander McFarlane gets to hear of me saying that, she thought.

Lydia blushed a fiery red.

'Yes, Mrs Helferty, I certainly will. Thanks for listening. I knew I could rely on you.'

So Lydia spent hours crouched on the stone floor of the jail, talking to Travis through the bars. The jailkeeper didn't seem to mind, reasoning that as long as the girl friend was there, the prisoner would stay quiet and refrain from causing a disturbance.

Under Lydia's sympathetic eye Travis was encouraged to talk, and he told her about his childhood in rural Ontario. His mother had died young, attempting to give birth to a little sister who had survived her mother by only a few hours. His father, a taciturn man, had never remarried but had given his boy a rough and ready upbringing.

He was a shoemaker by trade but owned a few acres of land which he farmed when he wasn't working in the shop. This meant that most of the burden of working the land fell on his young son, but Travis felt no bitterness over that, feeling that the experience had equipped him well for life as a prairie farmer.

The fact that they were both motherless made a bond between the pair.

'My mother died, too,' Lydia said softly. 'My father has married again, though, and Thea is nothing like my mother was. She can be rather horrid at times but my father doesn't see through her at all.'

'Is that why you came West?'

'Yes. I had to get away and marriage is the only acceptable way for a girl to leave home.'

For girls of your class, you mean, Travis thought.

Sadly, this confirmed his earlier realisation that Lydia was not wife material as far as he was concerned, which cut him to the quick because somehow she had got under his skin, as the saying went, and he loved her more dearly with each passing day. Not that it mattered, as things now stood.

'So that is why you answered the

advertisement in the newspaper,' he said. 'You were taking a chance, weren't you? And see what happened! You came all the way out here only to find that Joe Dunfield was already married. What a shock that must have been!'

'It wasn't wasted,' she murmured. 'If I hadn't come, I would never have met you.'

And how empty the world would have seemed if I'd stayed at home, never to know what love is, a small voice echoed in her head.

She held out a tentative hand, and Travis reached through the iron bars which separated the pair of them, and took the small, soft fingers in his work-calloused hands. They stood for some time without speaking, and then he drew her towards him and placed a lingering kiss on her waiting lips.

'I love you, Lydia McFarlane,' he whispered.

'I know,' she told him, and felt as though her heart was about to shatter into a thousand pieces.

12

Two things happened in the coming days to distract Lydia. The first was the return of Rose Dunfield, the other something totally unexpected which added to their burdens.

It was a Monday morning, and Frances was in the summer kitchen boiling a cauldron full of towels and sheets. The big wood stoves which did double duty in Canadian homes for both cooking and heating made life too uncomfortable in summer so most houses had another kitchen in a lean-to or separate shed which was used in the hottest months.

In spring and autumn there was always a great to-do about taking down the stove pipes and cleaning out the soot, before dragging the stove out to the summer kitchen or back into the house again. The small stove in the store had to stay put, year-round, for the purpose of making coffee to give to customers but by dint of leaving the door open and allowing cool air to come in, Frances was able to manage. An outer, screened door, kept flies and mosquitoes outside where they belonged.

Lydia was making fresh coffee, a task which she had learned to do under Frances's watchful eye, when the door burst open and a bevy of small children burst in, demanding sweeties. The tallest, a girl of about eight, dressed in a gingham dress and a stained white pinafore, pointed up to the glass jars in which Frances kept the peppermint sticks and candy.

'Do you have any money?' Lydia asked automatically, and the child's fingers uncurled to display a coin in her grubby palm.

'Momma pay,' a little voice said, and Lydia experienced a shock as she looked down on the tousled head of little Zachariah Dunfield, if that was indeed his name, as Joseph had been his stepfather, and a fleeting one at that.

So she was prepared for the unpleasant encounter that was to come, when Rose Dunfield, still covered from head to foot in unrelieved black, came through the door, accompanied by another woman who was obviously her sister.

Although her heart was thumping, Lydia managed to greet the two women quietly, and was somewhat relieved when the sister gave her a pleasant nod and smile in return. She was taller and plumper than Rose, and quite a bit older, but her homely features bore no sign of the strain which showed on her younger sister's face.

'Tell the girl what you want, Phyllis,' she told her daughter, and the next few minutes passed normally as Lydia took down bottles and weighed out the delicious contents, placing them in tiny brown paper bags.

There was a moment of disquiet as little Zachariah screamed his displeasure at being told he could not have a peppermint stick as well as pieces chipped with a tiny hammer from a slab of homemade toffee, made by Frances. Rose stood impassively by while her sister bent down and tried to explain that his money would only stretch to one or the other, but he was too young to understand.

Distressed, Lydia tried to pass a small piece of toffee to the child, being sure that Frances would agree that the circumstances warranted the gift, but Rose knocked her hand aside, frowning.

'We don't need your charity, miss! He has to learn. Unlike some, he doesn't have a rich father to cater to his every need!'

Sensing a coming storm, young Phyllis gathered up the other children and shooed them outside, where they could be heard shrieking and playing in the street.

'This is the young madam I told you about, Peg!' Rose sneered. 'The one that came from back East, trying to take my man away from me.'

This was so far from the truth that Lydia wanted to shout a denial, but she remembered in time what they had been taught at school — a soft answer turneth away wrath. Heavens knows it had come in handy many a time in her dealing with her father!

'I explained about the letter . . . ' she began, but her words were brushed aside as the woman ranted on.

'Now, Rose, is that fair?' Peg soothed, laying a hand on her sister's shoulder. 'Of course you've every right to be upset, after what has happened to you, but I'm sure this young lady isn't to blame.'

But Rose was in full flow now, and not to be stopped. Shaking off her sister's concern she continued to heap abuse on poor Lydia.

'Even supposing there was such a letter, and I'm not saying that there was, my Joe didn't write it. He told me that, plain as plain, and I believed him. If this person had showed up a few days earlier, she'd have married him though, and I'd have been out in the cold, as usual.'

'You've said all this before, Rose. You always did get all worked up, even as a child, always getting hold of the wrong end of the stick. How would this girl have known about Joe's existence unless there was such an advertisement in the paper in the first place? One way or another, she was brought out here under false pretences, and she's the one to be pitied in all this. He married you, didn't he?'

'Is that so!' Rose swung out wildly, managing to knock her sister's calico sun bonnet askew. 'Don't you dare take her side, Peg Harman! I don't know about all that and I don't care. All I know is that my man has been murdered, and I'm on my own again, with small children to raise. Oh, why do these things always happen to me?'

She began to sob, and, moved by pity, Lydia came round the end of the counter to see what she could do to help.

'Can I fetch you a glass of water, Mrs Dunfield? Or a cup of coffee, perhaps?'

The woman glared at her in such a threatening manner that Lydia took a step backwards before retreating behind the counter again, where she felt safe. Oh, why didn't Frances put in an appearance? She would know what to do!

Rose found her voice again.

'People like her have no right to come here, poaching the available men from honest women who have to marry again to find a roof over their heads. Fancy society ladies who've never done a day's work in their lives should marry their own kind. She should go back where she belongs, and I've seen to it that she's going to!'

'What do you mean by that, Mrs Dunfield?'

Lydia suspected what was coming next, but she had to know for sure.

'It was me notified your father,' the woman said, nodding in satisfaction. 'I saw the posters when I went up to Peg's place. I recognised you at once, so I went straight into the station and telegraphed him, like it said.'

'Why would you want to hurt me like that?' Lydia burst out, highly indignant at such a betrayal.

Rose looked at her as if she was mad.

'Because I thought there might be a reward, of course! A rich man, wanting to catch up with his runaway daughter would be glad to pay for the privilege, and I certainly need the money. If I hadn't turned you in, someone else would have done so, so why the fuss?'

Lydia looked at her through narrowed eyes. She might be rushing in where angels feared to tread, but she had to ask.

'You were the one who identified Travis Brown as the man who shot your husband, weren't you?'

'What if I was?'

'Well, can you be sure that it was Travis? It was late at night, and I'm sure you were terrified and desperate.'

Rose shrugged.

'It sure looked like him to me, and after I reported him to the authorities they found our cattle on his homestead, don't forget! That clinches it.'

'But there were two men. What became of the other one?'

Rose shrugged again, and, with a pitying glance at Lydia, Peg took her grieving sister by the elbow and ushered her out of the store.

When Frances came in, mopping her streaming face with her apron, she found Lydia seated on the stool behind the counter, deep in thought.

'Whoosh! I'm soaked to the skin with all that steam out there. Another five minutes at the washboard would have finished me off. Did I hear customers in here a while back?'

'Rose Dunfield is back, with her sister in tow,' Lydia said in a voice heavy with despair. 'She was the one who notified my father, in the hope of a reward. Honestly, I don't know which of them I'm the more upset with, Rose for being so spiteful or Papa for blanketing the country with pictures of me. Wanted, dead or alive!'

'Now, now, it's not as bad as all that, child. And as for Rose, you can hardly blame the poor soul. She's had a long row to hoe and seeing her new husband murdered was bound to throw her off balance. You must see that.'

'Perhaps, but I get the feeling that she isn't totally sure that it was Travis she saw that night. She just wants to put the blame on somebody. Her testimony is going to sway the jury, especially as the missing cattle were found at his farm, I know it will.'

'It always comes back to that,' Frances muttered, as if to herself. 'You could do with a change of scene, child.'

Lydia got up at once.

'Go to see Travis, you mean.'

'No, I do not! There's all that washing waiting to be rinsed and hung out to dry. Be a good girl and go and put it through the mangle, will you, and then peg it out on the line? There's nothing like hard labour to soothe a broken heart.'

Lydia did as she was told, and she soon found that Frances was right. She did feel better for being active, and as she watched the garments blowing in the breeze she felt a stirring of hope that all would come right in the end.

13

The worst thing they ever did was to allow that saloon to open up in town,' Frances grumbled. 'This used to be such a quiet little place, but now a decent woman can't walk down the street on a Saturday night without having to dodge out of the way of some drunken lout.'

'You'd think the saloon keeper would refuse to serve someone who seemed to have had too much to drink,' Lydia remarked.

'Huh! Not Bill Mackey! There's money to be made in drink, Lydia, and who is our Mr Mackey to turn away customers with cash to put down on the bar?'

'I shouldn't have thought that any of the settlers had any money.'

'Only if they've just sold some cattle, and the money is burning a hole in their pockets. Anyway, it's not just farmers who go to Mackey's saloon. There's all those travelling salesmen passing through, and staying the night at the boarding house. Not that Josie Drury would let them back in through the door drunk! Very strict, is Josie. Many's the time one of her lodgers has had to spend what's left of the night on the porch floor, after staggering home paralytic.'

'Then she'd have been out of pocket,' Lydia observed, but Frances only laughed.

'Not her! She takes in their money up front, ever since one fellow sneaked out at dawn without paying, after dining off the fat of the land, so to speak. There's no flies on Josie Drury, let me tell you.'

That night, there came a thunderous knocking at the side door, which served Frances as the main entrance to her house after hours when the store was closed.

'I'm coming, I'm coming!' she bawled, struggling into her robe and hastily arranging a kerchief over her hair curlers. 'Don't bust the door in!'

Fearful that they were about to be invaded by some of the saloon's customers, Lydia leaned over the banisters, ready to rush to Frances's aid if necessary.

Their caller was Tom Makinen. Lydia took a step down the stairs, afraid that something had happened to Travis.

'Come inside, man, do! You're letting the bugs in!'

He hastily stepped past Frances as she took a swing at a particularly persistent mosquito.

'Now, what's your problem, bringing decent folk out of their beds in the middle of the night!'

'Sorry, Fran, but there's a problem, and I don't know what else to do. There's been a drunken brawl down at the saloon, and there's a fellow hurt, unconscious. The doctor's been telegraphed for but they can't get hold of him. He's had to go out to the country to a birth the midwife can't handle. No telling when he'll be back, his wife says.'

'So what does that have to do with me, Tom Makinen?'

'We can't just leave him lying in the street,' he said reasonably. 'At any other time I'd have put him in the cell, but as you know I've already got a prisoner there. If this fellow came round and turned violent, they might do each other an injury, do you see?'

He turned pleading brown eyes on her, looking for all the world like a puppy begging for a pat. She laughed.

'And so you'd rather have the violence done to me, I suppose!'

'No, no, Fran. It's just that you had some experience nursing your husband before he died, and I don't know where else to turn. Josie Drury doesn't want to know.'

'She wouldn't,' Fran agreed. 'All right, Tom, I'll do my best for him, but I'm keeping the rolling-pin handy, mind, in case worst comes to worst!'

And so the stranger was carried in by two mildly-intoxicated men, breathing harshly, and laid out carefully on the sofa, on which Frances had prudently placed an old sheet.

'Just in case he loses control,' she explained.

Tom left, thanking Frances over and over again. The door closed, and they were left with the stranger. Lydia looked at him warily.

'Will we just cover him with a blanket and leave him there?' she wondered. 'Won't he feel uncomfortable with all his clothes on?'

'I doubt he's feeling anything just now,' Frances said. 'Not until he comes round, anyway. We'd better try to get him out of his suit, though. If you can prop him up I'll try to ease his arms out of the sleeves of that jacket.'

This proved to be something of a struggle because the poor man tended to flop in all directions. They managed to turn him on his side and, with Lydia supporting his head and shoulders, Frances got one arm out of his coat.

'So far, so good,' she puffed. 'Let's

flip him on to the other side now.'

Before long, they had removed the jacket and his collar and tie, and Lydia stood by, embarrassed, as Frances unbuckled his belt.

'Just you look the other way while I get his pants off,' Frances instructed, 'or better still, fetch a basin of hot water and some rags. We can at least wash some of the blood off his face before it hardens.'

Thankfully, Lydia scurried off. This activity was all very well for Frances Helferty, who had been a married woman, but she could well imagine what Alexander McFarlane would say if he learned that his daughter had been involved in undressing a strange man, unconscious or not!

When she came back into the room, she found that the man was lying decently covered with a blanket, with only his head and shoulders showing. He was still wearing his shirt, open at the throat. His collar had been of the detachable variety, fastened with a brass stud. Frances burst out laughing when she saw Lydia's expression of distaste.

'Don't you worry, child. He's still wearing his long johns. Neither of us will need to be embarrassed when he comes to! Now, dip one of those rags in the warm water and start sponging that cut on his head. Gently, mind! This is something else you need to learn if you're to be a settler on the prairie. Accidents do happen, and as we've already seen tonight, a doctor is seldom on the spot when he's wanted. You may have to deal with such things yourself.'

Lydia stepped forward, willing to do her best. She noticed that Frances was systematically going through the man's pockets, another invasion of privacy, but she held her tongue, knowing that the older woman was as honest as the day. Frances was looking inside his wallet now, nodding her approval of the number of treasury bills inside.

'At least we know he's not some sort of hobo, looking to thieve from people,' she said, 'although I can tell by his clothes that he's no pauper. Not wealthy, like your father, of course, but whoever he is he must make a decent living. And what is more, whoever it was that beat him up so badly mustn't have tried to rob him. I wonder what that was all about?'

'Perhaps someone came along before they had the chance to take his wallet,' Lydia said, wringing out the blood-stained cloth.

'Who knows? Say, here's a business card. This should tell us something about him.'

But all they were able to learn was that the man's name was Roderick Thomas, and that he was a traveller, representing a firm of men's shirts and underwear.

'I suppose if he hadn't been struck down he'd have been in here tomorrow anyway, trying to talk me into stocking some of these goods. Might have been a good idea, too. Save people having to send to the city for their winter clothing.'

They stood back, looking at their handiwork.

'Looks like he's not going to wake up any time soon,' Frances remarked. 'I'll sit with him tonight, Lydia. You go back to bed and get what sleep you can. In the morning, we'll talk about what we ought to do next. It all depends on what the doctor has to say, I guess, if he ever shows up.'

Wearily, Lydia did as she was told, and she fell asleep as soon as her head hit the pillow. Morning came all too soon, and after washing in cold water and tying a fresh apron over her working dress, she came downstairs to find Frances bustling about, preparing breakfast.

'How's the patient this morning?'

'Still out for the count. The station agent stopped by. The doc telegraphed to say he'll be here before noon, all being well. His horse is tired after going all the way out to the country and he wants to give it a rest. No point having it fall down dead in the middle of nowhere.'

'I should think not!' Lydia retorted, all her sympathy with the poor horse. 'What are you going to do next, Mrs Helferty?'

'I intend to get a bit of shut-eye while you mind the store. You can help me push two chairs together to make a sort of bed, and I'll settle down beside our Roddy, where I'll hear him if he stirs.'

So Lydia gobbled down her oatmeal and swallowed two cups of strong coffee in an effort to bring herself back to life, and went into the store. Surprisingly, there were no customers about for the longest time, until at last, just as she was about to doze off, the bell peeled and she looked up to see her father entering the store.

'Good morning, Papa!'

She waited to see if he had heard about their night visitor, but if he had, then he had something else in mind.

'I'll come straight to the point, Lydia. I've been making enquires about young Brown, from my business connections in Ontario.'

She jumped up, ready to protest, but he held up a warning hand and she subsided.

'I find that he springs from respectable origins, and nothing bad is known about him in the district where he was born and raised. It is true that the evidence against him looks black, but it would not be the first time that a man has been falsely accused. And this being the case, I have decided to bring out the best lawyer money can buy, to conduct his defence. Of course, this does not necessarily mean that he is innocent of the murder here, but that will have to be proven or disproven in court.'

Lydia's face grew bright with hope for a moment.

'If only he could have a good lawyer, I'm sure it would help, but I know he couldn't afford to pay the sort of fees such a man would charge. I'd do anything to help him, but I don't have any money, Papa. Mrs Helferty has been very kind, letting me work here in exchange for my board and lodging, but she hasn't paid me in actual money and I haven't liked to ask. Even if she could help, I don't suppose it would be much.'

Alexander McFarlane looked into his daughter's eyes.

'You say you'd do anything to help this young man. Do you mean that, truly mean that you'd do anything at all?'

Lydia nodded fervently.

'Then I shall be glad to pay the lawyer's fees if you will promise me faithfully to do one thing in return.'

'What is it, Papa?'

'If I bring this lawyer here, and underwrite the fees, and if, as we hope, the young man is let off, you, in return, will agree to come back to Kingston with me. If you really love him, you'll be willing to make this sacrifice. I'll give you some time to think this over, while I return to my coach. I'll expect your reply within the hour, which will be necessary if the lawyer is to be contacted and brought here in time.'

With a curt nod he left the store, the door closing quietly behind him.

Lydia began to shake. Like her father, she believed fervently that her word, once given, should never be broken. If she agreed to their bargain it might be Travis's only hope of going free, but then she would never see him again. Her father's words sounded in her ears.

'If you really love him you'll be willing to make this sacrifice.'

14

The court proceedings were to be held in the schoolhouse. The judge was due to arrive on the next morning's train. Whereas a magistrate or justice of the peace usually dealt with local criminals and meted out sentences, this was a murder trial and a jury would have to be sworn in.

Sad at heart, Lydia went to visit Travis for what might well be the last time. They clung to each other through the bars, and he whispered the words of endearment which she had longed to hear. But no matter what the outcome of the trial might be, she knew that it was too late for them . . .

'There's something I have to tell you,' he said suddenly.

'Yes, what is it?'

'It was me,' he said in a low voice. 'I was the one who did it.'

Lydia suddenly felt icy cold.

'Don't say anything more!' she begged, laying a finger on his lips. 'Somebody might hear. Don't you understand? It could be dangerous.'

'Dangerous? What do you mean, Lydia?' He gave a great shout of laughter. 'Don't tell me you thought I was going to confess to killing poor old Joe? No, when you hear what I have to say, you may feel like killing me!'

She was bewildered now.

'But what do you mean, then, about it being you?'

He looked down at his boots which gaped open because the laces had been removed. Tom Makinen had taken them as well as his belt in case the prisoner attempted to hang himself, thus depriving the authorities of performing the very same act, as the supreme punishment.

He took a deep breath and said, 'I wrote the letter to you, pretending to be Joe Dunfield.'

'What?'

'It was just a joke that went too far.

Me and some of the neighbourhood lads, we felt sorry for Joe, struggling all alone on that farm, never getting a proper meal because he had nobody to look after him. We kidded him about getting married, but he said he'd never been much for the girls and didn't know how to talk to them. We decided to put one of those notices in the paper, advertising for a wife for him. We thought that if anybody answered he could decide for himself what he wanted to do about it. He might find it easier proposing to a woman through the mail instead of face to face.'

'But when I answered, how did you come to see my letter instead of Joe?'

'As you know, all the mail comes here to the store, and people collect it when they come in to shop. Joe hadn't been in for quite some time, and Fran asked me if I'd mind dropping it off to him when I was passing by, in case it was something urgent. Trouble was, when I saw the letter with a Kingston postmark and the ladylike handwriting, I knew what it was, and chickened out.'

'And you replied to me instead,' Lydia said severely, remembering that beautifully poetic letter which had encouraged her to head West.

He hung his head.

'What I didn't know, until it was too late, was that Joe was going to get hitched anyway. He has a sister in Poplar Springs who knows Peg Harman, and knowing what a fix Rose was in, left alone with two babies to raise, they decided to matchmake. End of story.'

'Not exactly, Travis Brown! You drove me out to the Dunfield place, knowing full well what I was going to find.'

'I tried to talk you out of it,' he said, still looking very sorry for himself. 'I know I did an awful thing. Can you ever forgive me, Lydia?'

'Oh, yes, I forgive you,' she answered wearily, for what did it matter now? She and Travis were lost to each other. She might as well give him what consolation she could.

Two well-dressed and important-looking men climbed down from the train that morning. One was the judge, who had come in from Calgary, and the other the famous lawyer who had been summoned by Alexander McFarlane.

'We'd better retire to your coach and go over the case right away, Alex,' the lawyer said.

He had known Lydia's father for years and owed him a favour or two, which was why he had been prepared to drop everything to come West at a moment's notice.

'I'm curious to know what your interest in this affair might be. I didn't think you had any connections out here.'

'I don't,' McFarlane said stiffly. 'He's a young man my daughter has come to know very slightly, while vacationing here. She feels sorry for him and I agreed to help.'

Brian Curtin looked at him over the top of his horn-rimmed glasses, but said nothing. There was more to this than met the eye, but by the steely look on McFarlane's face he knew better than to probe further.

Once he had learned that there were two pieces of evidence against his client, the widow's testimony and the fact of the stolen cattle turning up on the Brown farm, he knew what he needed to do. His first stop must be the jail, to interview Travis, although that was likely to prove fruitless, and then he'd drop in at the saloon to see what people were saying there. If he knew country people and the way they liked to spin yarns, that would probably be a waste of time also, but he must be seen to be doing something towards earning his fat fee.

The next morning dawned clear and bright. People were streaming into town from all directions, eager to be part of the spectacle. From her bedroom window, Lydia saw a parade of mounted policemen, coming to take up guard outside the schoolhouse, in case there was any rioting, or an attempt to rescue the prisoner. At any other time she would have been thrilled at the sight of the red-coated men on their sturdy horses, but now they simply filled her with despair.

Travis had told her that no fewer than a dozen of them had turned up at his homestead to bring him in, almost as if they'd expected a shoot-out with an armed desperado. He had come with them meekly enough, knowing that to struggle would be completely useless.

Dozing on her makeshift bed, Frances Helferty woke with a start when she heard sounds coming from the couch where Roderick Thomas lay. Moving stiffly, she went to his side.

'Mr Thomas? Are you awake? Can you hear me?'

He looked up at her with puzzled blue eyes.

'Who are you, lady? What is this place?'

He struggled to sit up and fell back again, groaning.

'Just keep still, Mr Thomas. You've

had a nasty experience and you'd better not try to get up until the doctor has seen you. I'm Frances Helferty, the storekeeper and postmistress. Stay where you are, and I'll fetch the doctor to you.'

Luckily, she knew where the doctor was. He had come to town to meet the afternoon train, to collect his daughter, who attended a ladies' college in the city but was now coming home on vacation.

'Lydia!' she bawled. 'Run down to the station and fetch the doc. Tell him the patient has come to!'

The doctor was soon at the bedside, examining the patient and wanting to know what had happened.

'For I'm told that you were the victim of an attack. Have you any idea who the men were?'

Mr Thomas rubbed his hand over his eyes, frowning.

'It's all a bit of a blur, Doc, and I can't tell you their names because I'm not from these parts. Wait a minute, I'm pretty sure they were the same pair I heard talking outside the saloon. I'd gone along intending to have just one drink and no more. They tell me the lady at the boarding house don't allow guests who've taken too much, and I didn't want to get her upset. I don't sleep too well when I'm on the road, so a noggin helps me to nod off, see?'

'Do get on with it, man! I haven't got all day,' the doctor told him, not unkindly.

'These two fellows were drunk as skunks. What they said didn't make much sense, me being a stranger, but I couldn't help hearing something about what a joke it was, planting them cattle on some fellow called Brown.'

'What!' Frances and the doctor spoke at the same time.

'Did you hear anything else, man?'

'Well, Doc, they said it served him right on account of him taking the land they wanted. They'd waited a long time to get back at him, and boy, did they get their revenge this time. And then they saw me standing there and one shouted something about, 'Let's get him,' and 'If he heard something we can't let him go' and that's when they came at me, and not a blessed thing did I remember until I woke up here just now and saw the lady looking down at me.'

'The Parker boys!' Frances breathed. 'You remember, Doc. Those brothers from over Clariston way? Real outlaws, that pair. I wouldn't put anything past them. One of them had a piece of land near Travis's place and the other wanted the spread next to his brother, but Travis had already registered it in his own name. They tried everything to make him give it up, but he wouldn't do it. Said he'd spent months of back-breaking work clearing his land and he wasn't about to turn his back on that. It wasn't as if they offered to buy it from him, fair and square. They just wanted to run him off so they could take over. And they always vowed to get even.'

'Mr Thomas, I do believe you've had a lucky escape,' the doctor said. 'We might well have had two murders on our hands instead of one, maybe three, if they succeeded in getting Travis Brown hanged for their crimes.'

Lydia came running when she heard Frances' whoops of joy. She could hardly believe her ears when Frances told her the story of the Parker brothers and what Roderick Thomas had overheard. She turned to their patient, hardly daring to believe it, but one look at his beaming face convinced her that it was true.

'You're not about to faint, are you, lassie?' The doctor was smiling as he said it.

'Well, don't just stand there, child! Get going! Run over and tell that fancy lawyer what we've just found out. He'll know what to do next, I'm sure,' Frances said.

Grabbing her hat, Lydia dashed out of the house and flew down the street. There seemed to be more people about than usual, waiting for the excitement to begin, she supposed. Some gave her pitying looks, well aware of her link to the prisoner.

She wanted to shout at them all, letting them know that it was all over, that Travis would soon be free, but she knew she must be careful. If word got back to the Parker brothers that their victim had not only recovered, but was ready to give evidence against them, they might disappear for good.

As she sped past the jail she longed to step inside to share the wonderful news with Travis, but she dared not stop. Every minute counted. She could only imagine how he must be feeling, for justice moved swiftly out here. If he was found guilty, the sentence would be carried out within a few days, unless the judge permitted an appeal for clemency, which was unlikely.

She slowed down as she approached the siding. It wouldn't do to arrive panting and dishevelled. The last thing she needed was a lecture from her father about the proper demeanour suited to young ladies! She brushed down her jacket with her hands and pulled her hat down at a more becoming angle, tucking wisps of hair under the brim.

Inside the coach, Brian Curtin and Alexander McFarlane were taking their ease, relaxing in velvet-covered chairs, smoking cigars. Lydia was furious. Shouldn't Curtin be at the jail, preparing his client for the ordeal ahead?

'There's been a new development,' she said, aware that her voice had risen a few tones.

Her damp hands were clenched on the seams of her long serge skirt and her heart was racing.

'What sort of development?' her father asked, not stirring from his chair.

'That man Mrs Helferty took in and nursed. He's regained consciousness. The doctor is with him now!'

'Good. Good.'

'No, Papa, you don't understand! I mean, yes, it is good that he's going to recover, but that isn't what I've come to say. What I mean is, he says that two men called the Parker brothers tried to kill him to stop him talking. At least, he didn't know who they were, but Mrs Helferty says that's who they must be. He overheard them boasting about how they killed Mr Dunfield, and then took the cattle out to Travis Brown's homestead so the blame would be laid on him.'

'Why on earth would they want to do that?'

'Mrs Helferty can tell you all about it. She says it's a well-known fact that they've been holding a grudge against Travis because he won't give up his homestead land which they wanted for themselves.'

Her father grunted. Why, oh, why wasn't he taking her seriously? She shot an agonised look at the lawyer. Curtin had listened with interest, and now he stood up, stretching.

'I'll go and see what the judge has to say.'

He put on his hat, nodded to Lydia, and strode out.

'Doesn't say much, does he?' Alexander McFarlane said. 'He's got a good head on his shoulders, though, which is why I hired him. You get what you pay for in this world.'

'Will they let Travis out now?' Lydia asked anxiously.

'Perhaps not right away. It will be up to the judge whether to proceed with the trial, but I imagine that before any final decision can be made they'll have to apprehend these Parker men and see if there is any evidence against them.'

'And you'll never credit this,' Frances said, much later, when the Mounted Police had the two rustlers in custody, 'but they found those two idiots just down the street in the saloon! It seems they had every intention of going to watch the trial, to gloat over poor Travis!'

'I've heard tell of that before,' Roderick Thomas put in.

He was still being cared for by

Frances but was making great progress.

'Like people who set fires on purpose. Half the time they stay around to watch people fighting the flames, rubbing their hands with glee.'

The police had told him to remain in town until the Parker brothers were brought to trial, for his evidence was vital to the case. Lydia wondered what the jury would make of Rose Dunfield. Had she given false evidence against Travis, out of some misplaced spite against her rival, or was it an honest mistake, made under stress on a dark night? The jury would likely believe the latter, for what woman would not be flustered after seeing her man gunned down?

It was a very different Travis Brown whom Lydia went to visit in the jail that afternoon. The worry lines in his face had smoothed out, and he was clean-shaven, having been allowed to have hot water and a razor.

'The lawyer tells me I should be released this evening,' he cried jubilantly.

'The judge has to go over all the facts first, but everything points to the Parker boys now. It seems that when the Mounties caught up with them, Jed Parker was singing like a canary, blubbering about how it wasn't his fault. All he agreed to do was rustle a few steers. It was Jesse who gunned down Joe Dunfield. It was Jesse who drove the steers over to my place. In fact, to hear Jed talk, he was as innocent as a new-born babe throughout the whole affair.'

'He is an accomplice, though,' Lydia murmured. 'Will they hang him, too?'

'I don't know, and I don't care!' Travis said cheerfully.

Lydia joined Frances in preparing the evening meal, which included the cold dishes she was to take to her father, as well as to Travis.

'I guess that fancy lawyer will go back to where he came from now,' Frances remarked. 'Didn't do much to earn his money, did he, but no doubt he'll pad out his bill as much as he can.'

Lydia was silent.

'You're quiet, child. I thought you'd be dancing for joy now all this is over.'

'Of course I'm pleased, Mrs Helferty.'

'Pleased, is it! Something's wrong, I can tell. Come on, my girl, out with it!'

Lydia shrugged, and Frances thought she knew what the matter was. Talk about star-crossed lovers! The two still hadn't ironed out the difference in their circumstances. Well, if that was all that was coming between them . . .

'What will Travis do now?' she asked casually. 'Go back to the homestead and carry on as if nothing has happened?'

'I suppose so,' Lydia said dully and the older woman's heart went out to her.

'He still hasn't said he loves you, is that it? Some men just can't put those things into words, Lydia. They have to let actions speak for them instead. When you go over there with his dinner, just tell him you love him and you won't take no for an answer.'

'I can't, Mrs Helferty. I promised my father that if he hired a good lawyer to defend Travis, I'd go back to Kingston with him. Now I have to keep my word.'

Frances didn't know what to say. What a weasel Alexander McFarlane was to have presented his only daughter with such an awful choice! She had a good mind to march right over there and give the man an earful he wouldn't forget!

That evening, Travis was set free, and he and Lydia walked out to the edge of Cold Creek, hand in hand. There, under a rising moon, he took her in his arms and asked her to be his wife.

'I would have asked you long ago, sweetheart, but I didn't see how I could expect you to live in a sod house, after all you've been used to.'

'If you'd asked me then I'd have been willing to follow you to the ends of the earth, Travis. I'd have gladly lived in a tent in the desert if it meant being with you, but now it's too late. I have to go back to Kingston and I'll never see you again.'

It was too much for her, and she broke down and sobbed out her sad tale.

'Did he make you promise that you wouldn't marry me, Lydia?'

'No, but it amounts to the same thing, if you're here and I'm back there.'

'You didn't let me finish, my love. I've decided that farming isn't really for me, and I don't look forward to staying in a district where nobody but you and Fran believed in me when the chips were down. I have an uncle back East, my mother's elder brother, who is a well-known banker. He's written to me often, encouraging me to take a job in his bank, and that's what I plan to do now. You'll go home with your father now, and some fine day you'll turn up at the altar where a respectable young banker is waiting to marry you!'

So, after tearful goodbyes were said, Lydia took her leave of her good friend,

Frances Helferty, and climbed aboard her father's private coach, secure in the knowledge that the man she loved was seated farther down the train as they rode into their future together.

THE END